THE DEVIL'S RIDER

When vicious outlaw Jeremy Trask escapes the hangman's noose, he rides into Baton Ridge on a mission of revenge and bloodlust. It had been a year since he'd murdered manhunter Jim Darrow's brother in cold blood. Now, along with the sole survivor of the massacre, a young homeless widow named Spring Treller, Darrow vows to hunt down the outlaw — this time to finish him for good. But will he survive the deadly reception the outlaw has waiting?

LANCE HOWARD

◆

THE DEVIL'S RIDER

Complete and Unabridged

LINFORD
Leicester

First published in Great Britain in 2008 by
Robert Hale Limited
London

First Linford Edition
published 2009
by arrangement with
Robert Hale Limited
London

British Library CIP Data

Howard, Lance.
    The devil's rider - - (Linford western library)
    1. Western stories.
    2. Large type books.
    I. Title II. Series
    813.5'4–dc22

    ISBN 978–1–84782–850–7

Published by
F. A. Thorpe (Publishing)
Anstey, Leicestershire

Set by Words & Graphics Ltd.
Anstey, Leicestershire
Printed and bound in Great Britain by
T. J. International Ltd., Padstow, Cornwall

This book is printed on acid-free paper

For Tannenbaum

Please visit Lance Howard's
website at:
www.howardhopkins.com

1

The sun sinking into the distant mountains made the town of Baton Ridge appear awash in blood. Scarlet stained the encroaching shadows and sparkled from water in troughs like glittering blood rubies.

To Jeremy Trask, perched atop his horse, even the air smelled of the gunmetal scent of fresh-spilled blood. He could almost feel its silky wetness running through his fingers.

A prophesy, he reckoned, one that would be fulfilled in only a few fleeting moments. A fragmented laugh whispered through his thin lips. His scrubbed-gray eyes narrowed under a battered Stetson whose rim showed a hole where a bullet had punched through not two days ago.

He shifted in his saddle, nerves biting like fire ants under his skin, and glanced at the three others sitting atop their horses to his right. He'd reined them to a halt on the hill above the town, two men and one woman dressed in dusters and low-pulled hats. Each face held a look of vicious anticipation. These riders of his, they were as bloody a bunch as he had ever known, though anybody who knew him would have said they were greenhorns compared to their leader.

No, Pa, don't hit me anymore . . . please . . . I won't do it again, I swear I won't, I swear —

Pain stabbed his skull as a black memory echoed from the past. His gaze snapped back to the town, a surge of — what? Fear? Yes, it felt like fear that swelled in his belly. But not present fear. No, something worse, the kind that crawled from the depths of a fella's mind, made him relive the times a boy had cowered beneath a father's pounding fists; made him recollect the awkward and indifferent faces of folks in a town who had turned their back on a child, folks who had given up one of their own to a bounty hunter sent to bring in a bank robber.

Another whispered laugh escaped his lips. Had they only realized the true extent of Jeremy Trask's evil, known of the men he had murdered just because watching a fella bleed his last gave him pleasure, or of the women he had raped because nothing felt better than that moment of utter dominance over a weaker helpless creature; had they but known, they would have strung him up before that bounty man arrived and spared themselves the horror that would soon take place.

But they had not. And now their mistake sat on a hillside, a Smith & Wesson at his waist, a Winchester in his saddle-boot and a powerful rage surging through his veins. The time of reckoning was at hand. He was Fate's dark angel of vengeance.

'You sure we ain't better just heading out to New Mex?' came a voice beside him, shattering his thoughts.

Trask glared at the man, Decker, a tall angular owlhoot with dull green eyes. Decker had never been the brightest of his bunch, but he did what he was told, no matter how brutal or bloody.

'We got time for this . . . ' Trask's words trickled through teeth barely parted. 'We'll make the time.'

Decker shifted in his saddle, a tick stuttering near the corner of his lip. 'Just sayin' after breakin' you out the law's gonna be on our asses. Hell of a risk stayin' 'round these parts a'cause you got powerful mad over something that happened years ago.'

The rage within Jeremy Trask nearly grew overpowering then. It took every ounce of his willpower not to draw his gun and put a bullet through Decker's skull. But he couldn't rightly fault the man for stating the obvious and Trask knew he was likely right. It *was* risk. But that didn't matter a lick to him. What mattered was taking care of something he should have years ago, and punishing those who had seen fit to ignore the circumstance that had given birth to the man Jeremy Trask was today. What happened was as much the town's fault as it was that of his pa, Jacob Trask. And they would answer for it now.

'Man in town named Jacob Trask . . .' He paused, the name stabbing his innards. 'He's mine, you hear?'

'How we gonna know him?' the second man asked.

Trask glanced at Trompson, who was shorter, stockier, but smarter than Decker. Trompson's drawback was that his temper often fired a mite too quick, a trait that had nearly caused Trask to blow his brains out more than once.

'You kill him, I'll kill you, so you best figure it out 'fore you make the mistake.'

'I don't see how — ' Trompson started.

'Shut the hell up, Trompson. Now.' Trask cast him a glance that brooked no argument and the heavier man clamped his mouth shut.

Trask's gaze went to the third member of his gang, a young woman with chopped-off brown hair and sharp features who looked more like a boy. The duster, old trousers and loose shirt sure as hell didn't make her any more feminine.

'Get your skinny little ass down there, Trallie. Take out the marshal and any deputy you come across. We'll follow once we hear shootin'.'

She flashed him a grin, and he reckoned that if any member of his gang came close in viciousness to himself Trallie Hicks was just a notch south of pure badger. She let out a 'Yah!' and slapped her heels against the bay's flanks. He watched her charge down the hillside till she reached the outskirts of the town. The sun's scarlet rays bathed her and she became his blood herald, the harbinger of retribution.

Any fragments of fear in his soul dissolved in a rush of feverish anticipation and exquisite hate.

'I'm comin' for you, you sonofa-bitch,' he whispered. 'I'm comin' for you all.'

* * *

Days had blurred into an endless stream of hunger and fear. One after the other, with little or no food, nor modest comforts, rarely even a kind word. Nights were worse. Frozen nights huddled in the meager shelter of alleyways or broken-down campsites, soaked in fear and emptiness and hopelessness, the pathetic lot that had become Spring Treller's existence.

You can hate them, she told herself. *You can hate them all to hell and they'd deserve it, every last one of 'em.*

But hate was a waste of strength at this juncture, she reckoned. What use would it serve? It wouldn't change the folks who dwelled in Baton Ridge. It wouldn't change the hunger burning in her belly.

Arms wrapped about herself, legs

shaking, she wandered along the boardwalk. As her legs tangled in her skirt, which was torn in too many places to mend, even if she had been capable and had the tools to do so, she stumbled, righting herself by grabbing a supporting beam at the last second before going down. Hunger had weakened her and even walking the streets had become a nearly impossible task. She couldn't keep it up much longer. She needed food, even if she had to . . .

No, she couldn't do *that*. She couldn't allow herself to hate and she couldn't allow herself to throw away what was left of her dignity, the remnants of her pride. If she gave in, became one of *those* girls, her identity would be lost.

Oh, it would be so easy to accept the offers some of the town's men had made — food in exchange for an hour of her time, a measure of her womanly charms and sinful whispers. Until now, she'd spat in their faces, kicked a couple in their southern parts, then run. But now . . . now it was growing increasingly more difficult not to think about letting them touch her. With each passing day, each pang of hunger, each night spent with bugs and snakes crawling over her, she felt herself slipping towards the notion that had always repulsed her, the thought of becoming a whore.

How long had it been since her last meal? Dammit, she couldn't even recollect. A day? Two? A stolen apple from a cart, maybe it was. Was pride and morality worth starving to death? If she just joined the gals at the saloon . . . a place to stay, food, money would be hers.

All those *had* been hers not so very long ago. Three months, if she recollected right. With each day passing since the accident, things grew dimmer, but she reckoned that was only the confusion brought by fear and hunger.

A memory drifted into her mind as she pushed herself away from the supporting beam and began walking again. Her husband's memory, the funeral. She recalled the day the marshal had banged on her door, his face cold as the stone upon which they chiseled her man's name, and informed her Bill had died in a mine cave-in. She recollected the tears, the anger, the swollen emptiness.

She'd lost everything with his death. His love, their home, sustenance. No one in town had offered her help — well, no one but the barkeep, and that came with concessions. This town . . . they didn't protect their own. They cared nothing about a woman who'd lost her husband and was destitute; they cared nothing about anything that didn't directly affect their day-to-day selfish needs. They wouldn't care the day they found her body frozen in some alley, because once winter came . . .

You can hate them.

Or she could join them, perhaps. Give in. Become one of them and live only for herself and for what she could leech from their menfolk. Show those women who never offered a comforting word how she could pleasure their husbands in ways they never could, ruin their lives the way her own had been ruined. Take everything from those men who preyed upon grief for their own desires.

'No . . . ' she whispered, thoughts of doing things she'd sworn she never would crawling through her mind. But a body had to survive, didn't it? She had no skills other than what came natural.

It would be so very easy.

A tear slipped from her eye as again she remembered her husband, the kindness he used to show her, the way he worked so hard to provide them with the home the bank had seized two days after his funeral.

Maybe it would be better if you went to join him.

Lips quivering, she shook her head, nausea surging in her gut. 'You can't let yourself think that way,' she mumbled. 'Bill wouldn't want you to. He'd want you to get out of this town, find something better.'

But where could she go? Weren't all towns the same? She'd never seen different, and perhaps she'd even been one of those she had been struggling not to hate before circumstance had shown her being human was more than just taking, more than stepping over your neighbor's body the moment he fell because his carcass was in the way. Some lessons came hard, maybe too late, she reckoned.

No, you were never as bad as them, she assured herself. She'd always had compassion. She'd just suppressed it some, because there was never a chance of changing the way this town thought and behaved.

Maybe if she went to some place that at least had a church, maybe they would help her.

Or maybe they would just cast you out the way Baton Ridge has done.

A sob racked her body, which despite the lack of food was still full of hip and bosom. Tears streaked dirty tracks down her cheeks and she swiped them away with the back of her hand. She couldn't stand the confusion swelling in her mind anymore. She couldn't even make a decision to stay or leave or become another used-up whore. The simple things in life she'd once taken for granted were nothing but a horrible joke played on her by a God who never listened to the prayers of a young woman with nothing to offer but her body and nowhere to go.

She stopped, her mind jerking from her thoughts as she spotted a man standing twenty feet down the board-walk, eyeing her. He was probably headed for the saloon and in the gory light of the setting sun he appeared like some demon from hell come to claim her soul.

But he wasn't. He was just a cowboy, one she'd seen in town before. He might have even been one of the few to come to Bill's funeral.

He remained still, staring at her, the

13

sly look on his lips men only got when they eyed a woman with lust in their hearts.

Grin widening, he started towards her and she shivered. She wanted to shrink under his gaze, become a small helpless child begging a parent for a simple kindness.

'Please . . . ' she whispered, emotion making her voice quake as he stepped up to her. 'I need to eat. I need to eat . . . '

The man's smile changed and she could no longer tell whether it were sly or kind.

He tried to take her hand and she jerked it away, glancing up at him, then offered it to him as need took over. He took it, led her along the boardwalk.

'I'll feed ya — Spring, ain't it? I seen ya around.' The man was big, his hand calloused and gripping a little too tightly. His voice carried a booming eager quality she might have paid more attention to had she not been so desperate for food.

She nodded, her heart pounding in her throat. 'I just need a little help getting back on my feet . . . I'll pay you back, I swear.'

A peculiar laugh came from his lips, something predatory, like the hunter aiming at his quarry.

'I reckon you'll pay me first, you little whore.'

Before she could react he jerked her sideways off the end of the boardwalk and into an alley beside the café. She tried to resist, but her legs wouldn't work right and he yanked her along, his hands now gripping both wrists, his fingers gouging into her flesh.

'No, please, that's not what I wanted.' Her voice was barely more than a whisper, the horrible sensation of inevitability suddenly leaden in her belly. She would no longer have the choice; this man was about to tear the decision from her.

A spiteful uncaring laugh that might have come from the Devil himself fluttered from his lips.

'Didn't you? Don't all you whores want that? You expect me just to give you somethin' for nothin'?'

She struggled, but still couldn't pull her wrists free. It was all she could do to remain on her feet. 'I just wanted to eat . . . please . . . '

'Told ya I'd feed ya, but first you gotta do something for *me*.'

She shook her head, her mind swimming. 'I can't. I can't do that.'

He ignored her pleas, slammed her back against the wall of a building. She struggled against a cloud of blackness suddenly forming at the corners of her mind.

'This ain't right,' she mumbled, as if it would make a difference. Morality had died in this town ages ago. Perhaps it had never existed at all. At any rate, it wasn't about to flourish with an innocent young woman's pleas.

'Hell, it ain't!' the man said, spittle gathering at the corners of his mouth, his eyes eagerly aflame. 'Anything in this town's goddamn right. Even the goddamned marshal's got his hands in my business and everyone else's. We all take what we can get and that's the law of the land, missy. It ain't nothin' personal, just need. You think anyone will give you somethin' for free in this goddamn world you got another think comin'.'

And what of my needs? she might have asked, but didn't bother because fear had turned her innards to liquid. Her needs no longer mattered to anyone in this town and maybe now they didn't matter even to herself. This was going to happen and from there a door to others who offered her shelter and food in exchange for services rendered would open wide and beckoning. This act would banish temptation and make whoring nothing more than a deadened reality.

'Let's get you out of that blouse,' the man said, a laugh in his voice that disgusted her. She fought to pull his prying fingers away from the buttons of her top, but he got most of them undone, exposing the dirty chemise beneath.

'You can't do this,' she whispered. More useless words.

'It's already done, missy,' he said.

'Reckon it ain't.' A voice came from behind them, and at first Spring wasn't even certain she had heard it.

An instant later, as the man's head turned so he could look behind him, a shot thundered through the alley. His body jolted. A look of pain froze on his face and despite her own humanity she almost laughed. In his suddenly glazed eyes she saw a look of anguish and the reflection of one's own death and it was morbidly funny. She couldn't help it. Perhaps her mind had deserted her.

The man's fingers loosened from her blouse and he stumbled backward, then collapsed face first to the alley floor. He hit hard and she gasped, staring at the gory hole in his back that was acquiring an aura of scarlet.

Her own face a mask of shock, the horror of death sobering her, she looked toward the end of the alley to see a figure standing there, a smallish figure holding a smoking Smith & Wesson. The figure came deeper into the alley, stopped and glanced down at the body.

'He had it comin',' the figure said, and only then did Spring realize it was a woman, not a man. A masculine woman, in a duster and low-pulled hat. The figure's head came up and Spring saw sharp, boyish features and a look of detached coldness in her eyes. The killing had not affected this woman in the least. She might have even enjoyed it.

'Thank God you came,' Spring whispered, tears bursting from her eyes.

'Really?' the young woman holding the gun said, and Spring wondered about the hitch in her tone, and the sudden feral look sweeping across her face. In an instant she realized this was no avenging angel come to save her. This was something terrible, something perhaps even worse than the dead man lying at her feet.

'He was just about to . . . to . . . '
Spring's voice trembled.

'I reckon I know what he was about
to do,' the young woman said, nodding.
A smile oiled her thin lips. 'And I aim
to finish it.' The young woman lifted the
gun and drew back the hammer. 'So I
reckon you best continue undressing.'

★ ★ ★

At the sound of a gunshot Jeremy Trask
slammed his heels against his mount's
sides and sent the animal charging
down the hill towards Baton Ridge. His
hands tightened on the reins as hate
and rage swarmed over him. The two
other riders followed suit, a beat
behind.

Trask led his two men into town in a
rush of blood-colored dust and thun-
dering hoofs. One hand came free of
the reins, swooped to the Smith &
Wesson beneath his duster, drawing it.

Baton Ridge deserved to witness,

however briefly, a bloodbath like none that had gone before. No mercy, no regrets and no one left alive.

As they careened into town, the riders beside him drew their guns. They triggered shots at panicked men and shrieking women, sides of buildings, awning supports.

One woman's scream ended in a choked gurgle as lead plowed into her back and sent her sprawling forward to the boardwalk. She spasmed, making desperate strangled sounds, then lay still.

On the opposite boardwalk a cowboy staggered as a bullet tore through the back of his head. He tumbled over a rail and landed in a trough with a huge splash of blood and water.

With a splintering gunshot sound, an awning support buckled under a hail of lead. The awning crashed to the boardwalk, burying a cowboy, a shard of board running him through. The riders' laughs echoed through the streets, punctuated by gunfire.

Dust rose in great clouds, churned up by the gang's storming mounts, appearing glazed with scarlet from waning sunlight. Blood spattered the windows and walls of buildings, soaked into the dusty street, painted the corpses littering the boardwalks and ground.

How terribly fitting, Jeremy Trask thought, as he drew a bead on another cowboy and triggered a shot that jolted the man off the boardwalk and left him sprawled in the street. How terribly satisfying.

Three doors down a door popped open and the marshal flew out, a Peacemaker wavering in his shaking hand.

'Jesus Christ, Trallie,' Trask said through gritted teeth. That goddamn gal couldn't be trusted to put her own trousers on frontwise sometimes. A mistake like this might have gotten them all killed. Where the hell had she gotten to anyway? He'd heard a shot he'd figured was her signal, but there was the goddamned lawdog, gun in hand, headin' right his way, quite amongst the living. At least for another instant.

The marshal's gun swung up, aiming at Trask, though terror filled his eyes. He fully intended to blast Trask out of the saddle and Trask gave him credit for an ounce of balls.

Trask's gun swung in a fluid motion and his finger feathered the trigger.

The lawman staggered, lead piercing his belly, gun flying from his fingers. He stared up at Trask and Trask smiled, then put a bullet in the lawdog's face.

The screaming had started in earnest. Shouts and terror-filled yells crescendoed and the air was clogged with blue smoke and the acrid scent of gunpowder. Thunder from gunblasts echoed from buildings.

The good folk of Baton Ridge now realized something had invaded their town, something evil, a devil on horseback. And that pleased him, pleased him mightily.

Doors flew open as frightened men and women made a foolish run for safety instead of hiding themselves away. Jeremy Trask made sure they perished in mid-step.

The carnage lasted only moments and in some dark part of him he felt disappointment over that. The town was no more than one big sitting duck, but he had hoped to enjoy the slaughter longer. The sharp scent of blood and dust in the air, the shattered bodies, the destruction, none of it was enough. He needed to attend to one last piece of business before he could allow himself to feel completely satiated.

A half-hour later he and his men had raided nearly every shop and house and dragged broken bodies into the streets, strewn them across boardwalks, hanged them from awnings. Last came the saloon, where a few holdouts figured on making a stand, but they were no match for Trask and his two men. They butchered the last of the cowboys and most of the bar gals, except for two

24

whores his men dragged screeching into alleys for a bit of fun. Gunshots told him when they were finished.

Jeremy Trask waited in the street, standing amongst the dead and dying and blood dust.

'Where are you?' he muttered, scrubbed-gray eyes narrowed, inflamed with rage.

While most everything had gone as well as he'd planned — Baton Ridge had never been a town to stand up for itself, so it didn't particularly surprise him it should fall so easily — one thing hadn't. One man had somehow managed to save his own ass.

A man named Jacob Trask.

Jeremy Trask reckoned he shouldn't be surprised. The yellowbelly had likely pulled stakes the moment he got word his no-good son had escaped jail. Wasn't that just the way with bastards like that?

A grunt came from his lips, and with it a promise. A promise this was not over until his bastard of a father lay groveling for his life at his son's feet. Until that very same man lay dead.

'I'll find you,' he vowed.

A sound captured his attention and his head turned. Trallie strolled from an alley like she'd just walked out of a saloon and it pissed him off. The girl fumbled with the buckle on her trousers and he could damn well bet what she'd been doing.

'Where the hell you been?' he said, when she reached him, a flop-eating grin on her face. 'You were s'posed to take out the marshal. You mighta got us all buried.'

She made a *pfft* sound that irritated the hell out of him. Something was goddamned wrong with that gal, he reckoned.

'Had me some business,' Trallie said. The smugness in her tone only annoyed him the more.

'That business dead now?'

Trallie looked down at her dirt-crusted fingernails. 'Pret' near.'

'What the hell do you mean, 'pret'

near'? She's dead or she ain't.'

'Reckon she's breathing her last. You know how I like to beat 'em after.'

Trask gave Trallie a small nod, then looked down at the Smith & Wesson in his hand. Like a scream in darkness, his rage rushed back. Just like that. And just like that his hand snapped up and the gun butt clacked off Trallie's jaw with the sound of boards slamming together.

The young woman collapsed, struggled to push herself back to hands and knees. Blood ran from her mouth, and her eyes appeared glazed. 'Goddammit, Trask!' She spat a stream of saliva and blood into the dirt. 'Why'd you go and do that?' Her eyes cleared and she glared up at him, murder in her gaze.

'I'm gettin' goddamn tired of you not followin' orders, Trallie. Consider this your final warning.'

He walked off, leaving the girl drooling blood and spit. He felt a mite better.

2

'I should have killed him, little brother.' James Darrow forced back the tears welling in his eyes and struggled to swallow the ball of emotion lodged in his throat. He knelt before a small headstone in the cemetery just outside of Orchard Pass, forearm draped over one knee, Stetson dangling from his fingertips.

'Now he'll be out in a couple years . . . ' He gritted his teeth and lifted his head to stare up at the sapphire sky. Christ, it should have been easier coming here after all this time but on this day, exactly one year after Clay died in a bank robbery, pain still burned a hole in his heart and made him want to lash out at everything and everyone.

Wrong place, wrong time, folks had told him, as if that were some sort of comfort. Clay had done nothing to get himself killed other than to be in a bank to deposit their manhunter earnings when that gang had busted in.

Clay wasn't supposed to die first. He was younger, the one with a bright future. From what came out at the trial, Clay, impetuous as ever, had made a fool move and tried to stop the four-member gang from harming some woman he didn't even know and gotten himself in the way of a bullet.

Life wasn't goddamn fair. And at times a bitter side of him wanted to blame the woman Clay had saved, but he knew it wasn't her fault. Clay was a hero, the papers had said, as had the woman, who spent most of her time on the witness stand crying. Although she had testified the men all wore masks, she had pointed out the leader as Clay's shooter based on build and eye color.

But the bullets that killed Clay and three others hadn't matched the leader's gun and some fancy frocked-coated lawyer from the East had nailed his case shut with that fact.

Four people had died that day yet the man responsible had escaped with only a sentence for robbery.

But Jim knew better. That bastard had killed Clay. Didn't matter which gun the bullet had come from. The sonofabitch was responsible for his gang's actions, a gang Jim had spent a year tracking without a kernel of success.

Whatever the case, that man had killed before; Jim had seen murder in the outlaw's gray eyes. That man . . . that man was as bad as they came. But Jim had thought, foolishly, the day he was sent to bring him in justice would be served. He had relied on a system he saw growing increasingly more fickle as the West became ever more domesticated. Wasn't right. Some men, men like the outlaw responsible for Clay's death, would never be tamed, could never see the error of their ways or suffer a moment's regret. They took whatever they wanted, regardless of the consequences or the pain it caused others. Men like that . . . only way to deal with them was to put them down like a rabid dog.

Jim had made a wrong decision and now he was forced to live with it, while that man sat in a jail with the possibility of being set free in a few years to kill again. And Clay lay in a grave, his body rotting, his soul restless.

Is it his soul, Jim? Or your own?

Clay was at peace; the minister had told him as much. Only Jim Darrow burned with the unquenchable anger and restlessness, the grief that refused to be quelled by a man of the cloth's platitudes and practiced reassurances.

But how could Jim Darrow rest knowing that outlaw would someday kill someone else's brother or loved one?

'Christ, Clay, I'm sorry,' he whispered. 'I should have killed him. Even if it damned me to hell I should have killed him. I swear he walks out of that cell I will.'

He could hear Clay chiding him, way he had always done when they rode together on cases. Clay may have been his younger brother but Jim reckoned the little pecker had been born more world-wise. ''Course, I got all the looks,' Jim used to taunt back. A ghost of a smile came to his lips with the memory. It quickly vanished.

Clay would tell him killing that man when he went free would only result in his own hanging, and plenty to answer for to St Peter when he got to the Gates. But Jim Darrow reckoned he'd stopped believing in Heaven and angels. Now he only believed in loneliness and loss, and a God of vengeance.

Jim reached out, his trembling fingers drifting across the chiseled name on the headstone. A tear slipped from his eye and he shook his head, trying to force the pain away. 'Goddammit, Clay, why'd you have to go and get yourself killed?'

He rose to his feet, fist clenching.

'Goddammit!' he screamed at the empty sky. Only the sound of the breeze rustling leaves left over from the previous autumn reached his ears. Then the twittering of some bird in the forest beyond the cemetery. And the ghostly whisper of his own heartache in a forgotten graveyard.

Past was the past. Nothing he could do about it right now but when that sonofabitch walked out of jail, Jim Darrow would be there, waiting. With one bullet.

'Don't back talk me, Clay,' he whispered, wondering if he weren't going a bit loco talking to a brother who couldn't hear him. Wondering if he hadn't lost his mind the day he found out his only kin had died.

Did it matter?

His hand slipped into his coat pocket and he pulled out a small silver flask. He plucked off the cap and took a long drink of the contents. Whiskey burned its way to his belly but failed to chase away the fury in his heart. It never did and he supposed he should have long ago stopped expecting it to do so.

After returning the flask to his pocket, he set his Stetson atop his head and turned from the gravestone. He reckoned he planned on getting blind, raving drunk in the saloon so he wouldn't have to spend the rest of the night thinking on his brother's death. What the hell else was there for him now? He hadn't taken a case in the last year. He might as well spend more time feeling sorry for himself.

'You ain't the first to lose a brother.' How many times had he told himself that? How many times had it failed to quell even a small measure of his grief?

A sound reached his ears, drawing him from his melancholy. His gaze traveled beyond the rusted iron gate to the trail that led to Orchard Pass. His brown eyes narrowed to a squint. A rider was approaching the boneyard, a young woman.

'What the hell?' he mumbled. In as

many times as he had come out to this place no one had ever ridden up. Few in town visited this cemetery unless they had to.

The rider drew up outside the gate, had trouble dismounting because of the ripeness of her belly. Once on the ground, she tethered the reins to an iron rail.

'Tessy?' he said, as she stepped through the gate and came up to him. He knew her from town, knew her husband, John, in passing. Nice folks, he reckoned, young, starting their lives. But the distress on her face made something in his gut cinch.

'Jim,' she said, in a rush of breath, then paused to breathe more deeply. She peered at him and he knew she saw something in his own eyes that took her aback for an instant. Grief had a way of spilling itself on others.

'What's wrong, Tessy? You look like you seen a ghost or something.'

Her young face had drained of color and strands of blonde hair hung loose from the tight bun to wisp about her face. Redness from crying streaked her blue eyes and dark pouches nested beneath them.

'No, it's just John . . . I'm powerful worried.' She placed her hands on her swollen belly, smoothing out the wrinkles in her flowered yellow maternity dress.

The tight feeling in his gut worsened. 'John? Why, what's happened to him?'

'Maybe nothin', maybe I'm just jumping to conclusions, way the marshal said, but I got an awful feelin' in my gut, Jim, and I reckon I don't know you well enough to ask you no favors, but I got no other choice 'cept ridin' out there myself and with the baby comin' . . . '

His gaze went to her distended belly, the child likely only less than a month away.

'Reckon you're takin' a chance ridin' in your condition,' he said, more out of worry than reprimand.

'I know . . . ' Her gaze dropped as

she kicked at a twig on the dusty ground.

He tried a smile, but it came hard. 'S'pose you tell me what you think happened and just try to calm down a bit, 'fore I have to carry you all the way to the doc's.'

She nodded, her lower lip quivering. 'It's just, you know John does some freelance work for the bank. He goes to surrounding towns once a week, stays for a couple of days. But each morning he telegraphs me, lets me know things are OK and that he loves me. I ain't got a telegraph in two days.'

His brow crinkled. 'Maybe there's some line trouble or something and he can't get a message out. There could be a hundred possible explanations, Tessy. You're gettin' yourself worked up over nothin'.' But even as he said it he didn't quite believe it himself. He had no reason not to believe it, but something inside him, something dark that might have birthed the day he found out Clay had died, told him a storm was coming and with it would be suffering for this young woman.

A tear slipped from her eye as she shook her head. 'I tried to tell myself that, I really did. I ran through every possible explanation and in my mind I know there ain't no reason to be gettin' this worried. But in my heart . . . ' Her gaze probed his and the pain within it somehow reached into him, burned. 'You ever had just a dreadful feelin' somethin' powerful awful has happened to someone you love? A feelin' for no reason, you just *know* it?'

Oh, Christ, he knew the feeling. Goddamn intimately. He'd felt it the day Clay died. 'Reckon I do. You ask the marshal to send a man out, check on John?'

She nodded. 'He said what you did about lines and other explanations. Told me to wait a few more days and if John don't come back then he'll send someone down there.'

'Maybe you should wait then — '

'I can't! I can't wait that long. I got

this young 'un comin' and I can't even stop crying long enough to do my chores. He's all I got, Jim. Please, I'm beggin' you to go down there and check on him. I ain't got much money but I know what . . . what you were. You were one of the best and I'm willin' to give you everything I have.'

He sucked in a deep breath. 'I ain't tracked in a year, Tessy. I dunno . . . '

She clutched his forearm, her bleached fingers digging deep into his muscle as if she were clinging to a log in a raging river. 'I know you suffered a loss. And I know you know what it feels like to miss somebody so much you feel like your heart's just goin' to burst clean out of your chest. And I know I'm probably gettin' riled 'bout nothin' and I'll go myself if I have to, but I got to know John's all right. Please . . . please help me.'

He swallowed, reckoning his evening getting pie-eyed was going down the drain and wondering if riding out searching for a wayward husband while dealing with his personal ghosts on the anniversary of Clay's death was the smartest idea. But the look in her eyes . . . Christ, he couldn't say no to that and if she hurt herself or the baby he'd never be able to live with himself. He had enough guilt to carry around.

He nodded, a half frown on his lips. 'I'll take a look for you, Tessy. Probably nothin', though, so please try to calm down and get yourself some rest. I'm sure I'll have him back soon enough. And save your money. You'll be needin' it soon enough with the young 'un arriving.'

More tears rushed from her eyes. 'Thank you.' She grabbed him, hugged him tight and the feeling of her distended belly pressing against him made him feel damn peculiar in a way he would have been hard-pressed to explain. Something about the beginning of a life mingled amongst so many passed in this boneyard.

'Where did he go?' he asked after she pulled back.

'Baton Ridge. He had business there.'

The name froze him. Darkness washed across his eyes and he knew she saw it.

'What's wrong?' She wrapped her arms about herself, shivering.

'I . . . nothing. Just that town . . . got some bad memories of it.' It took him another full moment to regain his composure and when he did he wrapped an arm about her shoulders and guided her back towards her horse. 'Let's get you back to town and take the ride a bit easier this time. We don't want you droppin' that baby halfway back. I ain't the midwife sort . . . '

★ ★ ★

Two hours later Jim had seen Tessy Cambridge back to her homestead and assured her three more times John would be OK and back home with her before she knew it. There had to be a perfectly reasonable explanation for his silence.

But a niggling voice in his mind told him different. Perhaps it was something associated with that devil town he was on the trail heading towards, or perhaps it was the gut feeling all manhunters experienced that warned when some tragedy or life-altering event lay waiting at the end of the line. Whatever the explanation, he felt certain of one thing:

John Cambridge was dead.

He tried to convince himself the feeling was merely an echo of what he had felt the day Clay died, mixed with the memory of riding into Baton Ridge to bring back the man whose gang was responsible. But the dread swarming through him wouldn't accept that explanation.

He sighed, shifting his rangy, six-foot-one frame in the saddle, the big bay beneath him snorting and jouncing with every dip and rise in the hardpack. His hands tightened on the reins, going white with strain as he gripped too tightly.

Hell, it's just getting to you, Jim, the

anniversary, the prospect of riding back into that town, the notion this is your first mission in a bit over a year . . .

On a strong horse, Baton Ridge was only a couple of hours' ride from Orchard Pass and he'd already traversed three-quarters of the way, but with each mile that slipped behind him his mood grew darker and the notion he was going to have to tell Tessy bad news more certain.

He forced his grip to relax, knowing he was working himself up over maybes. Whatever awaited him in Baton Ridge, he would know shortly and his qualms would either be borne out or dismissed. Until then speculation was useless.

Holding the reins with one hand, he drew the flask from his pocket and took a deep drink. Liquor burned but did little to chase away the dread. He shoved the flask back into his pocket and his gaze steadied on the trail ahead.

The day had warmed and he'd shed his coat. Sweat soaked the sides of his bibshirt and his heart pounded more than he would have liked.

In an unconscious gesture, he touched the Peacemaker at his hip, then returned his hand to the reins. Being back in the saddle was harder than he had thought it would be. He'd gotten used to wallowing in his self-pity, ignoring jobs that came his way. Everything felt somehow awkward, detached.

For the past year he'd given little consideration to going back to man-hunting. It just wasn't the same without Clay at his side. Everything seemed emptier, darker.

Without thinking, his head turned, as if he somehow expected to see his brother riding beside him, expected to engage his younger sibling in one of their good-natured arguments or hear that barrel-chested laugh of Clay's that usually scared birds out of trees for half a mile.

A smile touched his lips.

'I miss you, little brother. Just ain't the same no more.'

44

He focused on the trail ahead, emotion choking his throat and tears welling in his eyes.

Twenty minutes later, he reined his mount to a stop and sat on the hill overlooking Baton Ridge, every dark feeling in his belly solidifying. Minutes dragged by as he struggled to breathe. Sweat ran from his brow and streaked down his sides and chest, despite the fact a chill washed through him.

'Jesus,' he mumbled, gaze transfixed on the town's wide main street. He'd expected a rush of feelings upon seeing the town again, but nothing like the horror that swelled within him now.

A shudder pulled him from his shocked trance.

Something terrible had happened, something beyond his immediate comprehension and worst nightmares.

Half in a daze, he gigged his horse into a funeral gait down the hill. With each hoof fall, dread and horror became more acute. For maybe the first time since the murder, he felt thankful

Clay was not here to see what met him in the streets of Baton Ridge.

The town was a shambles. Awnings canted, some shattered and completely collapsed. Bullet holes riddled shop walls and numerous windows had been blasted out. Doors hung open, mute testimony to lifelessness.

But the worst sight was the bodies. Everywhere. Bodies lay all around, covered with blood, with tortured frightened expressions. Strips of flesh and eyeballs had been plucked free by the buzzards that scattered as he came through the wide main street. Those carrions would be back soon enough to finish their gruesome job.

Some corpses hung from awning beams by makeshift nooses fashioned from belts or twisted bonnets, while others lay in pools of dried blood in the streets or splayed on boardwalks. Not a one stirred. He did not have to be a crystal gazer to know none would ever move again. Only the whispers of the dying haunted what was now a ghost-town.

Shaking, he swallowed hard, everything inside him screaming and recoiling from the sight. He wanted to look away, banish the image from his mind, but could not. The gory sight held him transfixed. He'd never seen the likes of such butchery, such wholesale wanton murder. No Indian massacre ever did as thorough a job of killing.

An entire town, from the looks it. Gone. Wiped from the earth. He saw no feathers, lances, nothing to indicate some passing band had attacked. No, Indians weren't responsible for this slaughter. Whoever had struck this town wasn't a man. It was a monster, a force of evil incarnate.

He reined the bay to a halt and slipped from the saddle, barely aware of his actions. His legs shook as he guided the animal to a hitch rail and tethered the reins. The bay nickered, shifted feet, the scent of rotting death permeating the warm air making it nervous. His own belly clawed its way into his throat. He suddenly leaned over, hurling his stomach contents into the dust.

'Aw, Jesus . . . Jesus,' he said between retching and gasps. Sweat streamed from him now, drenching his shirt and stinging his brown eyes. A convulsion of horror racked his muscular frame.

When at last he straightened dragging moments later, he had regained only a measure of his composure. He doffed his hat, wiped sweat from his brow using his forearm, then returned the hat to his head.

Forcing himself to go on, he stepped on to the boardwalk and headed to the first body he saw. A marshal, face frozen in death, maggots crawling over his flesh. Another burst of nausea almost made him lean over the rail, but he managed to control it this time, his mind partially numbed by the sight of so many dead.

His gaze traveled further down, noting more bodies sprawled in troughs and hanging over rails, others splayed halfway through building doors, their outstretched fingers frozen into claw shapes.

He drew deep breaths, legs getting a bit steadier as he walked. This was a vision that would never leave his nightmares. In his ten years in man-hunting he'd never encountered the likes of such carnage; it would stay with him to his dying day.

He stopped, gaze rising to a form dangling by a noose from a supporting beam a handful of yards down. For a frozen moment he didn't move. The corpse confirmed his worst suspicions.

'John . . . no . . . ' He forced himself to move again, go to the body. Sweeping the Bowie knife from his boot sheath, then holding the body about the waist with one arm, he sliced through the rope. He lowered the corpse to the ground as gently as possible, then returned the knife to its sheath and bowed his head. What the hell was he going to tell Tessy now? He'd assured her everything would be all right, but it wouldn't be, would it? John Cambridge would be coming back to her, but not in a way any young wife with child would have ever wanted him to. Their child would never know its father.

He knelt beside John Cambridge's body, pulled the flask from his pocket and downed the rest of its contents. The whiskey didn't help. He hurled the flask in a burst of rage and screamed, 'Goddammit!'

Moments trickled by, his belly churning, his mind racing, searching for any possible reason such a horrendous event could have occurred, why someone should lay waste to an entire town, but explanations eluded him. It was loco, plumb loco.

'What the hell happened here?' he said, through gritted teeth.

He tried to focus on reasons again, possible clues, but emotion overwhelmed him and he just knelt there over John Cambridge's body, head in his hands, unsure what to do next, which way to turn.

One of the best, Tessy had called

him. What a hell of a joke that was. 'You picked a hell of a horse to get back on . . . ' he whispered.

A gunshot shattered his spell and his head jerked up. A bullet had torn splinters from the supporting beam from which he'd cut down the body of John Cambridge, only inches above his head and to the left.

Christ, someone *was* alive in this town. And that someone had just missed taking off his head.

His instincts flowed back like he'd jumped on to a familiar mount. Without further thought, simply a firing of nerve and muscle, he scuttled sideways in a crouch to the back of wagon parked near the boardwalk, getting behind it.

Another shot thundered; the bullet missed him by more this time, but still came close enough to send a chill down his spine.

His hand swept toward his waist and in a liquid blinding motion his Peacemaker was poised beside his cheek as if it had materialized there, his finger feather-light on the trigger.

Another shot. A chunk of wood splintered as lead punched through the wagon and kept going to bury itself in the boardwalk.

He rose, exposing himself momentarily, chancing two quick shots in the direction from which he judged the bullet had come — an alley diagonally across the street. He expected to hit no one, merely put whoever was shooting at him on notice he wasn't going to be the easy prey the others in this town had been.

As a fourth shot answered his salvo, he ducked back down.

One person could not have caused this much carnage, could not have butchered an entire town without being taken down, even with the element of surprise; whoever was shooting at him was one person, so this was either a lookout left behind or a frightened survivor. He was willing to bet on the latter, since no one had picked him off the moment he rode in.

'Who are you?' he yelled.

A scream came on the heels of his question. A woman's scream. Other noises followed, the sound of feet dragging in the dirt. He risked peering around the wagon and spotted the shooter, then. A woman, all right. She was staggering into the street from the alley, a gun straight-armed in her hands, aimed at the wagon. Those hands shook and he reckoned had they been steady her first bullet would have splintered his skull instead of the beam a few moments ago.

As she came closer, his gaze narrowed, focused on her quivering form. Her dirty blonde hair hung mostly loose about her grime-smeared features, which might have been lovely under other circumstances. Dirt streaked her face and bruises and welts shown on her high cheekbones and jaw line. Her lips were swollen and her clothing torn, blouse hanging half open, exposing much of her breasts. She fumbled at the edges of the blouse with one hand, trying to cover herself, while barely able to hold the gun out straight before her with the other. Blood had caked about her lips and nose and her eyes were blackened, one half closed.

A stumble almost sent her to the street. He wasn't entirely sure how she stopped herself from going down.

This was no killer, he reckoned, though if he gave her a chance she might become one.

A few steps closer and he glimpsed something in her eyes, pure terror mixed with some other dark emotion.

'Bastard!' the woman screamed, the gun wavering and he was afraid she would start triggering shots again. He didn't want to wound her but might be forced into it to preserve his own life.

'Miss, please, I'm not your enemy!' he yelled at her, and she cackled as if she'd gone plain loco.

Letting go of her blouse, her free hand went back to the gun to brace her aim and she triggered another shot that tore shards from the wagon.

'Come on out, you sonofabitch!' she

screeched. 'Come on out and die like a goddamn man!'

Five bullets, he told himself. She had fired five times; she had one shot left. If he could get her to discharge it without perforating him maybe he could talk some sense into her.

He risked exposing a bit more of himself, straightening from behind the wagon. 'Miss, I ain't responsible for what happened here. I came to help.'

She uttered another cackling laugh and he wondered if what she must have been through hadn't unhinged her. 'Nobody helps anyone but themselves in this town . . . '

She stopped, faltering, gun lowering a few inches. She appeared exceptionally weak, both emotionally and physically.

He took a chance, stepping out from behind the wagon, but ready to dive sideways should she jerk the gun up.

Her eyes flashed a look of hate and determination. With what little strength she had remaining, she hoisted the gun and fired.

Had he not dove sideways with her first motion, lead would have drilled through his chest. The slug buried itself in a wall behind him, but at least now the threat was over. She had fired her last bullet.

The recoil kicked her backwards a half-dozen feet this time, but somehow she managed to hold on to the gun.

He came around the wagon and terror flashed over her dirty features. She pulled the trigger; an empty clack sounded and that terror strengthened. She fired again and again and each time the hollowness of the hammer hitting made the fright in her eyes swell.

He stepped off the boardwalk, walked slowly toward her. 'Miss, please, I'm not going to hurt you . . .'

She gazed at him with spite, then hurled the gun at him. He sidestepped and the weapon landed in the dirt a few feet away. The move seemed to sap the last of her willpower. She collapsed to her knees, a sob racking her body.

He paused, standing before her,

emotion swelling in his throat. A moment ago she had been a threat to his life, a frightened animal backed into a corner. Now she appeared nothing more than a fragile pathetic thing, lost, defeated.

'Please . . . ' she mumbled, looking up at him, tears streaming down her dirt-streaked face. 'Please just kill me this time . . . '

He shook his head, a pained expression coming on to his features. 'Miss, I'm not going to hurt you. I came here looking for a woman's husband after he didn't contact her and I found' — he glanced around at the bodies scattered everywhere — 'this.'

Her eyes said she neither believed nor disbelieved him, only that all hope and fight had deserted her. Now only surrender remained.

He knelt before her, his brown eyes sympathetic and searching. 'What happened here, miss? Who killed all these people?'

She shook her head. 'I . . . don't

know. They came, riders, and one of them . . . ' She broke down, tears flowing harder, body shuddering. He noticed she had no shoes and tears in her skirt showed she had nothing but shreds and bruises covering her legs. Someone had beaten her nearly to death.

'Miss, please, who did this to you?'

Sobs shook her body and for long moments she remained silent before looking up again, dullness now in her eyes. A gauntness and redness to her face indicated more than just the experience she'd suffered at the hand of whoever had ridden into this town. Likely she been exposed to the elements and not eaten for at least the past few days. She was on the verge of blacking out and he feared if she did she might not regain consciousness again.

He sighed. 'When's the last time you ate anything, two days, three?'

'Longer.' Her voice came a mere whisper.

He straightened, leaned over her, reached out. She made a move to resist, then gave up and let him take her in his arms and lift her. He carried her towards his horse, her body feeling frail, nearly lifeless. Whatever strength she had left she'd used in trying to kill him.

He reckoned the bodies in the town were going nowhere and nothing would change until he got back to Orchard Pass and informed the law of the tragedy. Getting food into her first was more important, or the town would claim another victim.

When he reached his horse he set her on her feet. She wavered, clung to the saddle to keep from falling.

He fished a length of jerky from his saddle-bag and handed it to her. After she devoured the dried meat, he gave her his canteen and she gulped at it.

'Not too fast, miss. You'll make yourself sick.'

A moment later, she doubled over, struggling to hold on to her belly. He took the canteen from her, waited until she managed to straighten without vomiting.

He gave her another piece of jerky and mounted, then hoisted her up behind him. The food and water would help hold her until they got back to town and he could buy her a decent meal. They could talk about what had happened in Baton Ridge after she got some of her strength back.

Reining around, the girl's arms wrapped about his waist, he cast a last look at the carnage in the town and fought nausea from rising in his own belly again. Whoever had done such a horrible thing would pay for it, he told himself. Whoever had left this girl here to die would answer for the crime. He had a year's worth of rage on deposit and he reckoned he aimed to spend it liberally.

3

Jim had watched Spring Treller — she'd finally told him her name an hour out of Baton Ridge — devour a huge beefsteak, two baskets of biscuits and a pot of coffee in little under twenty minutes. Halfway through her second slice of cherry pie, her head down, blue eyes riveted to the food, she jammed the fork into the desert and shoveled a heaping bite into her mouth.

While he waited for her to finish, his gaze traveled about the small café in Orchard Pass, noting a handful of folk occupied tables covered with blue-checkered clothes and adorned with fresh-cut wildflowers. The waitress had given him an uneasy look upon seeing him enter with Spring, whose soiled and torn clothing and grimy appearance raised a number of eyebrows from the other customers as well. But he reckoned the girl's appearance was secondary to getting her strength back and the fastest way to do that was to feed her. She'd tied the front of her blouse closed with a string the waitress had provided, which at least got his own mind off things it should not have been on — he was a man, after all. Jim spent most mornings in this café for breakfast, so any objections the management might have broached never materialized, though the occasional askew glances from the other patrons were getting on his nerves.

It's just this day and all that's happened making you over-sensitive, he told himself, taking a deep breath.

Judas Priest, what kind of monster did something so heinous? All those people . . .

He glanced at Spring, hoping she trusted him more now and would soon feel free to talk about what occurred in Baton Ridge, at least provide some small lead to whoever had raided the town. Beyond telling him her name, she'd remained silent the entire journey.

Her head lifted, her blue eyes, still red, holding more pain and sadness than he had ever witnessed on another human being.

'I'm ready,' she said, setting the fork on the plate, pie finished.

He cocked an eyebrow, noting an odd note of submission in her tone. 'Ready for what?'

'You can take me to your place or wherever you want me to . . . *provide* for you. I won't fight it no more.' Her voice shook and he studied her dirt- and bruise-blemished face, which now carried a bit more color.

He leaned back in his chair, brow crinkling. ''Fraid I still don't get your meanin', miss.'

The smile she gave him came without emotion and laced with cynicism. 'Nothin' comes free, mister.'

'Told you my name was Jim.'

She frowned. 'Nothin' comes free, Jim. I learned that these past few months. 'Specially from menfolk. You fed me, reckon you expect somethin' in return. I can't fight anymore. I'm too tired. You've won.' A tear trickled down her face and she shuddered.

'You aren't beholden to me for anything, miss.' He folded his arms across his bibshirt. 'All I want is for you to tell me what happened in that town and who did it.'

A puzzled expression flickered across her battered face. 'Why?'

'Because I aim to find the men responsible and make them pay for what they did.'

She shook her head, went silent, as if she were struggling to keep her composure. 'That's not what I meant. I meant, why don't you want something from me? Every fella in Baton Ridge wanted something from me when they offered me food or shelter.'

'Baton Ridge.' He hesitated, darkness washing over him with the mention of the name. 'Baton Ridge is a town peculiar unto itself, Miss Spring. I saw that a year ago when . . . ' The words stuck in his throat. 'Well, not every town is like that one nor is every fella the same as those who live . . . *lived* there.'

She studied him, the first spark of life he'd seen in her making her eyes a softer blue. Cleaned up and stripped of that terrible sadness, he reckoned she'd be a lovely young woman. She still didn't trust or believe him, he could tell, but just maybe she had begun to relax her defenses a bit.

'I told you I don't know who did it.'

'Let's start with you, then. When's the last time you ate before today?'

She shrugged, gazed out the window decorated with saffron café curtains. 'I . . . four days, maybe, five . . . and just a heel of bread, then.'

'Five days? Nobody in that town offered help?' Disgust rose inside him.

Her face darkened with sadness again as she looked back to him. 'Sometimes the general store owner gave me scraps, but I reckon he was hoping to wear me down till I was beholden to him. Others were more direct, but mostly I stole what I could. I'm no thief but I didn't have a choice. I figured it was better than — '

'Sellin' yourself.' He frowned.

She nodded, the bleak emotion on her face deepening. 'My husband . . . he was killed in a mining accident. Bank took our home. I've been on the street since. Only other choice was the one the 'keep gave me and I couldn't make myself do that. I told myself once that happened I didn't have any part of me left, but now it doesn't matter.'

'Does matter, miss. This town isn't the same as Baton Ridge.'

'Ain't just the town.' More tears washed down her face. 'One of them . . . one of them raped me . . . '

His belly sank and he turned away from her, swallowing hard, then looked back, capturing her gaze. Emotion nearly overwhelmed him. Everything that had happened this day, combined with the anniversary of Clay's death . . . it was damn near too much. And now this young woman . . . someone had defiled her, despite the hardship she'd been through. Someone without a lick of compassion or mercy and it infuriated and sickened him.

'I'm going to find them, Spring. I'll make them pay for what they did to that town and to you. Just because someone took something by force doesn't mean you got an obligation to give it against your convictions.'

She laughed, the sound pregnant with pain and lost naivety. 'You'd be surprised how quickly a body's convictions waver when you're faced with a devil you can't fight.'

He wanted to say that it wouldn't surprise him, that he knew a thing or two about unconquerable devils, because just a year ago he would not have considered killing a man in cold blood. Now . . . now if the fella who'd murdered his brother walked into the café damn little could have stopped him from putting a bullet between the bastard's eyes.

'Tell me what happened, best you recollect,' he said instead, his heart heavy.

'I . . . I was hungry. A man, one of the fellas in town, he came along the boardwalk, offered me food but he wanted . . . he dragged me into the alley. He was going to take me, but another shot him, killed him, then . . . '

He nodded. 'He did what the first aimed to do.'

'He?' Her gaze went distant, confusion and hurt and disgust washing across her features in waves.

'The man who raped you, Spring,' Jim said, running a finger over his top lip.

'Oh . . . yes.' She nodded, looked out the window. 'Left me for dead, too. Beat me something awful and I had no strength left to fight. Reckon *he* thought I would die in that alley soon enough.'

'But you didn't. You take the gun you

68

used on me off the dead man?'

She nodded, looking back to him. 'I'm sorry, I didn't know.'

'You couldn't have after what you went through. You saw a threat and tried to protect yourself. Can't hold that against you.'

'I was in that alley for two days, just lying there. I remember . . . I remember cold at night and darkness, then the heat of the sun and . . . pain. Then I heard a horse, your horse. I forced myself up and grabbed his gun. I could hardly lift it. I saw you standing over a body.'

He nodded, belly sinking. 'A young woman asked me to go to Baton Ridge to look for her husband. That was him. I ain't lookin' forward to telling her.'

A shudder racked her body. 'No . . . I know how she'll feel. Same way I felt the day they told me . . . told me my husband was gone.'

'You're positive you have no idea who raided the town? Did you see or hear anything that would point me in a direction?'

She shook her head. 'I heard horses, yells, screams. And gunshots. So many gunshots.'

He frowned, then reached into his pocket and pulled out a wad of greenbacks. He tossed a few on to the table and returned the roll to his pocket. He stood, grabbing his Stetson from the table and setting it on his head, then offered Spring his hand. She accepted it. Her hand felt somehow as fragile as a child's.

He peered at her, trying to make his expression comforting, confident, to reassure her he was not after anything from her in return for whatever he provided.

'I'm going to ask you to do something you may not be able to do, Spring. I'm going to ask you to trust me, at least a bit. I don't expect anything from you in return, you have to believe that.'

She nodded, defeat back in her eyes.

'What difference does it make? What can you do to me that hasn't already been done?'

He spent the next hour having the doc check her over. She'd been lucky; she was bruised and battered but no bones were broken and she appeared to have no internal injuries.

After, he took her to the hotel and set up a room, open-ended, for her. They stood in the lobby after the hotel clerk had passed her a key.

He placed a number of greenbacks in her hand and closed her fingers about them. 'You take these and get yourself some clothes, then come back here. I'll have the hotel man send up a bath so you can get yourself cleaned up. I'll make sure you got food until we figure out how to get you on your feet.'

A hint of a smile crossed her lips and tears shimmered in her eyes. 'Why are you being so kind? You don't know me and I tried to kill you first thing.'

'You've been through hell. Ain't hard to see that. You just need a chance.'

'I reckon I've been taught I don't deserve kindness from anyone.'

He gave her a reassuring smile. 'You've been taught wrong, Spring.'

She nodded and he watched her leave the hotel to find the dress shop. He hadn't told her the full reason he wanted to help her. He'd failed to be there the day his brother died. He was damned if he would let an innocent woman perish because fate had seen fit to piss all over her.

After arranging to have a bath sent up to her room, Jim left the hotel and headed along the boardwalk. The marshal's door popped open and the lawdog stepped out, a peculiar look on his face. It was plain he must have seen Jim ride in with Spring and had been waiting for him to finish his business.

But down the street, walking towards him, was another woman, anguish on her face, and something in his heart withered. He signaled off the lawman, who nodded upon spotting the woman. He would speak to the marshal in a bit.

First he had the devil's task to perform and he wished to hell he didn't have to be the bearer of more tragedy and suffering.

Tessy Cambridge came up to him, tears already running down her face. She knew. Somehow. She had known when she sent him to look for her husband.

He held her in the street for what seemed like endless hours but was probably only a handful of minutes. She sobbed into his chest until two women he recognized from the church came over and took her, guiding her away. He would talk to them about Spring later, he reckoned, see what they could do for the young woman.

Hat in hand, he stood watching them take her away, emotions welling within him that ran the gamut from rage to crushing sorrow. Christ, why was the world filled with so much pain, so many monsters? Why would some all-powerful God see fit to play with lives like they were nothing more than dying leaves cast about on the wind?

He wished to hell he knew.

He turned and went to the board-walk, then walked up to the marshal, Dan Mason, who still stood outside his door, his face somber.

'John?' the lawdog asked, already knowing the answer.

Jim shook his head. 'And worse.'

The marshal gave him a sober nod. 'You best come inside. Likely even what you got ain't the whole of it.'

He nodded, sighed, followed the lawman into the office, leaving the door open behind him.

He lowered himself on to the hardbacked chair in front of the desk while the marshal poured himself a cup of coffee from a blue-speckled enamel pot on a small table.

'Coffee?' Mason offered and Jim shook his head. He'd had a cup at the café and right now his belly was churning too much to put down anything else.

The marshal, a few years younger

than Jim, but with touches of premature gray in his hair and chimney sweep mustache, lowered himself into the seat behind his desk. He leaned back and took a sip of his coffee before setting the cup on the desk.

'What happened?' the lawdog asked.

Jim swallowed hard, tossed his hat on to the desk top. 'Whole town's gone, Dan.'

The lawman's eyes narrowed. 'Gone? What the hell you mean, gone?'

'Someone rode in and wiped it out. Killed everybody. Bodies lying in the street, hanging from awnings, dead in buildings. All shot dead. John Cambridge was unlucky enough to be there when it happened.' The images flooded his mind, making his belly churn even worse.

The marshal shuddered, took a deep breath and remained silent a moment, as if struggling to process what Jim had just told him. 'The girl you rode in with — '

'Only survivor. One of them raped

her, left her for dead. But she doesn't know who did it. She only saw the fella who forced himself on her, I reckon. Maybe we can get a description out of her on that account later, but she's too shaken up to press right now. She's been through a lot, even before this, apparently.'

'Ain't likely you'll need a description.'

Coldness washed through Jim with the look that came into the lawdog's eyes. 'I don't like what I'm hearin' in your voice.'

The lawdog shook his head. 'I reckon I'm powerful sorry, Jim.' He opened a drawer and pulled a yellow slip of paper from within, then tossed it across the desk to Jim. 'This came in from Barterville an hour ago. I read it over three times and still can't believe it.'

Jim's eyes narrowed and he plucked the slip from the desktop. An instant later everything inside him froze. 'Jesus . . . Trask . . . '

The marshal nodded. 'He escaped a

few days ago with the help of that gang of his we were never able to find. Then someone robbed the bank there. They all wore masks but I got a notion it's too big a coincidence not to be him. I reckon he needed to pick up some quick cash. Killed the marshal there; he was a good friend of mine.'

Jim pressed his eyelids shut, took a deep breath, then opened them again. 'I'm sorry, Dan . . .'

The lawdog waved him off. 'We all are. Reckon I don't have to tell you the connection Trask has to Baton Ridge, seeing as you're the one who brought him in.'

Jim let the telegraph slip from his fingers on to the desktop. No, the lawdog *didn't* have to tell him. It wasn't something he'd ever be likely to forget.

'Trask . . . you reckon he's responsible for what happened in Baton Ridge?'

The marshal nodded again. 'That's my first thought but I don't know for sure — '

'No. *I* know for sure. Same way I know for sure he killed my brother, no matter what that fancy lawyer said at the trial.' Jim stood, rage searing through his veins at the thought of the outlaw loose. Here was his chance, the one he'd been contemplating, having nightmares about for a year. He could hunt the sonofabitch down and kill him. And God forgive him for the bastard thought that he was almost glad the man was free, though the death and pain and sorrow he'd caused a short few days made him feel immediately guilty for the notion.

The marshal rose from his seat, nodding. 'What do you plan to do? You haven't ridden out after anyone in a spell.'

'All the same, I'm goin' after him. I'm goin' after him for killing John Cambridge and for what he did to that town and that young woman I rode in with.'

The lawdog studied him, searching Jim's eyes. 'You're goin' after him for killin' Clay. And you ain't plannin' on both of you comin' out alive.'

Mason was right. No use denying the obvious. 'Then I best make sure it's Trask who gets fitted for a pine box.'

'I'm going with you and I won't hear no objections.' The lawman came around the desk, put a hand on Jim's shoulder. 'That marshal in Barterville was a friend; I owe him that.'

Jim nodded.

'I'm goin', too,' came a voice from behind them and both men turned. Spring Treller stood in the doorway. She wore a new riding skirt and crisp tan blouse. She'd scrubbed the dirt from her face and pulled her hair back into a ponytail, and despite the bruises and welts on her face she struck Jim as one of the loveliest women he'd ever seen.

The marshal shook his head, distress flickering in his eyes. 'Ma'am, this fella we're plannin' on huntin' down, if he did this to Baton Ridge, he's near kin to the Devil himself. We can't let you risk your life again. You've been through enough from the sounds of it.'

She came deeper into the office, her lips drawing into a hard line, her eyes narrowing with conviction. 'What I was made to do in that alley . . . ' Her words came low through gritted teeth, laced with hate and disgust. 'It was unnatural. I aim to see to it that happens to nobody else. This fella you're talkin' about, he butchered my entire town. You try to stop me I'll go after him on my own.'

Jim studied her, a measure of confusion sparking. 'I understand why'd you'd want the fella who raped you, Spring, but that town, they never gave a damn about you. Why do you care what happened to them?'

She turned to look out through the large plate glass window into the street. With a shudder, she wrapped her arms about herself. 'Whatever they did or didn't do for me, they were people. They deserved somethin' but not what was done to them. And that man from this town who was killed . . . I saw you tellin' his wife. She's with child and now she'll face what I faced when I lost my own husband. Only it'll be worse for her because of the baby. Reckon I had given up on everything, was about to let myself do something there was no turnin' back from. Now, if I got a choice, I choose to help, because nobody helped me until you came along.'

'I don't like the notion of a woman comin' along after a dangerous outlaw,' Mason said, face dubious.

'I can shoot near as well as any man,' Spring said, turning back to them.

Jim nodded. 'Reckon I can testify to that, Dan. She damn near perforated me 'fore she knew who I was.'

Something close to a smile flickered across Spring's lips. 'Then where do we find this sonofabitch you were talkin' about?'

* * * *

'Where the hell's Decker?' Jeremy Trask asked Trompson, who sat across from him at the small rickety table in the ramshackle cabin. 'He shoulda been back by now. I sent him for supplies over five hours ago.'

Trompson shrugged. 'He had to be careful. Ain't likely no one would recognize him from the breakout since we killed most everyone, but you never know. He's got a wanted poster on him for somethin' he did while you were in the hoosegow. Always a chance some lawdog might get lucky.'

'Ain't what I wanted to hear, Trompson.' Trask slapped down his cards, suddenly bored with the poker game, then came to his feet. Scrubbed-gray eyes narrowing, he peered about the draughty mining shack where they had holed up, a few miles outside of Baton Ridge. The dump contained little more than a table and some bedrolls, scattered cans of beans and a battered coffee pot, but it was ample shelter for the time being. A work table was nailed to the south wall; it still contained various pieces of equipment for separating silver from rock — small hammers, dishes designed to hold mercury, used for amalgamation, jars and bottles. The law wasn't likely to find them here and there was only one trail in so chances were they would see them coming.

Irritation crawled through his nerves at his missing man. Decker should have been back with better supplies at least two hours ago. Christ, he'd warned that stupid sonofabitch to be careful and purchase only what they needed for a few days, so no red flags would be raised. If that goddamn peckerwood had gotten caught and led the law back here —

A laugh interrupted his thoughts and Trask's gaze swung to Trallie Hicks, who poised at the mining bench, a bottle of mercury in her hand and a damned peculiar look on that boyish face of hers when she glanced back at him. The look only served to irritate him further.

'Somethin' you find particularly

funny about the situation, Trallie?' he asked, irritation singing in his voice.

She let out a small chuckle, turning her gaze back to the bottle in her hand. 'Just recollectin' the taste of that woman on my lips, that's all.' She gave him a sideways look that made his skin crawl. Weren't many things Jeremy Trask could say turned his belly but Trallie Hicks had managed to find one of them. He reckoned she got some kind of goddamn odd satisfaction out of it, too. She was pushin' her goddamned luck.

'Christ, you make me sick, Trallie.' He spat on the dirt floor.

'Don't I, though?' She didn't bother turning to look at him. A whimsical quality to her tone didn't calm him any. She went silent, poured some of the mercury into a small dish, then watched it shimmer.

'You know that goddamned stuff's poison, don't ya?' Trompson said, looking back at Trallie.

A chuckle. 'Ain't everything?'

'Let 'er drink the goddamned stuff, if it suits her,' Trask said, annoyance bleeding from his tone.

Trompson uttered a mean laugh. 'Hear tell it's a bad way to go . . .'

Hoofbeats sounded before his temper stepped another notch and he decided to slam her face into a wall. He went to a window, peered out. ''Bout goddamn time.'

A few minutes later Decker stood in the cabin, two canvas bags of supplies he had toted in with him propped in a corner.

'What the hell took you so long?' Trask asked, gaze locking with Decker's.

Decker's face took on a guilty expression and a nervous tick stuttered near his mouth. 'Went back to Baton Ridge to make sure we left no loose ends. After what you told me about Trallie leavin' that girl to die I figured it was a smart thing to do.' Decker cast a glance at Trallie, who returned a sneer.

'Pussy,' she said, looking back at her

dish of mercury.

'You what?' A bolt of fury sizzled through Trask's veins. 'Goddammit, Decker, I told you to be careful. That town's probably crawling with lawdogs by now. If you led anyone back here — '

Decker's tick stuttered faster and he shifted feet, licked his lips and swallowed hard. 'Christ, give me a chance to explain, Trask. I didn't lead no one here. There was only one fella there, that bounty man who brought you in a year ago.'

'Darrow?' Surprise lashed his face. That was a name he hadn't expected to hear again. 'What the hell interest would he have in a dead town? His job was done when he hauled my ass in.'

Decker shrugged. 'Maybe he figured out you switched guns with me after killin' his brother.'

The blow came without warning. A backhanded fist clacked from Decker's jaw and the outlaw stumbled backward and slammed into a wall. The entire shack rattled with the impact and for an instant Trask thought the whole place might come down on them. Trallie uttered a maniacal laugh and Trompson sat frozen at the table, eyes wide.

Trask stepped over to Decker, intent on putting a boot in his teeth, but the outlaw held up a hand. 'Please, Trask, I didn't mean nothin' by that. It's a damn good thing I went back, though.'

'Why's that, Decker?' Trask backed off, some of his rage siphoning.

Decker shot a look over at Trallie, whose back was still to him, then looked back to Trask. 'He was lookin' around that town and some woman tried to kill him.'

At the bench Trallie stiffened, turned her head towards Decker, a glint of worry sparking in her dark eyes.

'A woman?' Trask didn't like the notion he was getting and flashed Trallie a spiked look.

Decker nodded, getting to his feet. 'Yessum, came out of an alley and shot at him, but she missed. She ran outa bullets and collapsed, but he helped her. I followed them back to Orchard Pass. Looks like someone from Darrow's town was visitin' when we rode in. We killed some pregnant gal's husband, now I reckon Darrow's got an itch to find out who did it. I could see it on his face. And that woman, looks like she's got a bigger itch. She's powerful peeled at somethin'.'

'At somethin' . . . ' Trask mumbled, glancing at Trallie. He made a disgusted sound, looked back to Decker. 'Don't much give a damn about a woman but Darrow . . . he had it in for me the moment that lawyer got me out of havin' my neck stretched. I could see it in his eyes. He reckoned on killin' me one day. I'd damn near forgotten about him.'

'We should head for Old Mex, Trask.' Decker maneuvered back a step, as if worried Trask wouldn't take the suggestion without violence. 'Darrow's going to come after us and this time there won't be no jail — they'll hang us.'

Trask shook his head, struggling

against a wave of rage washing through his innards. 'No. We don't leave until I pay my father a visit.'

'But — ' Decker started, shutting his mouth the moment Trask flashed him a look.

'You and Trompson get out of here. Don't come back for an hour.'

Decker nodded and scrambled for the door. Trompson was out of his chair and outside only a beat behind him. Trallie started to step away from the bench.

'Not you, Trallie. You stay.'

For one of the few times he could recollect a glimmer of worry danced in her eyes. 'Reckon I should go with 'em — '

'I said, you stay.' Trask kicked the door shut and walked over to her like a man approaching a funeral. He plucked the hat from her head and tossed it backwards on to the table. She was boyish, but not entirely ugly, he reckoned. She still had all the parts a man needed to satisfy himself.

'Reckon you told me you left that woman for dead.' Accusation laced his tone.

Trallie backed up a step, pressing her rear against the bench. Trask doubted the woman was scared of *any* fella, except him, and her eyes reflected the fact she had made an error for which she was going to pay dearly.

'I did. I swear she wasn't gonna walk out of there on her own. Hell, she's was damn near fallin' down when I got hold of her.'

'Yet she was strong enough to take shots at Darrow.'

Trallie shook her head, her face reddening a notch. 'She didn't see nothin', Trask. No way she can lead him back to us.'

'She saw *your* face, Trallie. But I reckon it won't matter none anyhow. Won't take Darrow long to put it together once he finds out we broke out. That's the only thing keepin' me from puttin' lead between your eyes.'

Relief came into Trallie's eyes. He

knew it would and it pleased him. It would make what was going to happen next even sweeter.

'Then we're done, Trask?' She tried to slip sideways. He slammed a hand against the wall, trapping her.

'Oh, we ain't even close to done, Trallie.'

'But I thought it didn't matter that girl saw — '

'It don't. But you didn't do what I told you to do. That mighta got us all killed and I'm goddamn sick of you not followin' orders.'

'I will from now on, I swear, Trask. I will.'

He almost laughed. He could see it in her eyes she never would, not unless he broke her like a goddamned wild horse.

'You ever been with a man, Trallie?' he asked and she started.

She blinked and he swore if he didn't know better she might have been holding back tears. But not Trallie. Trallie never cried like some ordinary female. She was too much a fella for that.

'Just . . . just once,' she whispered. 'When my ma's fella took me when I was a young un'.'

'What you do now, it ain't right, Trallie. Ain't natural for a woman not to be with a man.'

'What difference does it make to you?' she spat back, defiance and spite suddenly flashing in her eyes. There. That was more like it. And it annoyed the piss out of him.

His hand came up in a sharp arc, taking her across the jaw. Her head rocked like carriage with a bad spring and blood ran from her lips. He laughed, then jammed his lips to hers. She struggled, but he was too strong and she was suddenly too scared. Didn't matter she was as tough, likely tougher, than any man he'd laid eyes on. *All* bent to Jeremy Trask's will. All cowered beneath the fear he'd been taught to instill, the very fear he'd suffered himself by his pa's hand until a bit over a year ago.

He drew back, gaze raking her. 'We're gonna do this, Trallie. We're gonna do this and you're gonna goddamn like it. I'm gonna set you straight about what's right and wrong 'tween a fella and a gal.' He laughed at the stark terror that washed across her face.

Then he grabbed her by the shirt and hurled her on to a bedroll and began to unbuckle his belt . . .

4

Fifteen years ago . . .

The fist struck Jeremy Trask's jaw like a bolt of lightning cracking from a rain-bloated sky. Bone collided with bone with the crash of thunder. He flew backwards, slammed into the wall of the small shack he and his pa called a home and slumped to the floor.

'Git up, you no-good yella bastard!' his father yelled, the words slurred and liquidy. A webwork of blood stained Jacob Trask's gray eyes and spittle bubbled at the corners of his mouth. But the worst thing was the promise on the old man's face, the promise that assured a twelve-year-old boy he'd be lucky if this time the monster he called his pa didn't kill him.

The elder Trask poised there, waiting, a vulture of pain. He rubbed his busted knuckles on his stained and torn undershirt, a man of nearly forty, chin salt and peppered with stubble, nose veined by whiskey and eyes completely devoid of compassion. A monster, sure as any that ever came from the tales told 'round a blazing camp-fire on a moonless night.

A monster of fear and hurt, driven to pound all sense of humanity from a child he'd never loved, never wanted.

Jeremy, his entire body shaking like a newborn calf, pressed his hands back and used the wall to push himself back up to his feet. His legs wanted to give out, but he knew if he let himself fall his pa would only make it worse and use his feet to kick the hell out of him instead of his fists.

Ringing pain rang through his teeth and jaw and he wondered if his pa had fractured a bone. It wouldn't be the first time. How many times had his pa told the sawbones his clumsy son had been thrown from a horse or fallen off a fence? Too many for Jeremy to recollect. He suspected the doc knew better, suspected the whole town knew better, but they never lifted a finger to stop it.

At first he had reckoned they were simply as afraid of his pa as he was himself, but over the past year he had come to learn that wasn't the case. Baton Ridge wasn't a'feared. They simply didn't give a damn. It wasn't their problem and a blind eye turned let them live with themselves. What was one young boy to them? What business was it of theirs interfering in the God-given right of a father to discipline his child?

He spat out a stream of blood and saliva that filled his mouth and knew instantly he'd made a mistake. Rage flashed across his pa's eyes and Jacob Trask stumbled closer, grabbing his son by the collar and hoisting him up against the wall. The impact jarred his senses, and for not the first time a rush of unbridled hate surged through his innards. He wanted to kill his pa, take the old shotgun on the wall-rack above the fireplace mantel while the old bastard was sleeping off his whiskey, ram it into his mouth and pull the trigger.

But as many times as the thought had occurred to him he had never been able to go through with it. The fear that man had beaten into him prevented action, paralyzed a boy with the belief that somehow the man might return from the grave to torment him for all eternity.

'I'm sorry, Pa,' he mumbled, voice bloated with terror. 'I didn't mean to do it.'

'Christa'mighty, you never mean to, do ya, boy?' Jacob shook him and everything inside felt as if it had been rattled loose. 'McMurdie in town told me you stole a goddamn peach from his store.'

A tear slipped from Jeremy's eye. 'I was hungry, Pa. You ain't been home in two days.'

'I always come back, don't I? You know I go to Lockeville every fifth of the month, then come back in a day or two.'

Jeremy shook harder, tears now streaming down his face. He cursed himself inwardly for being such a coward again. But what else could a boy his age do? He had nowhere to go and none of the folk in town would take him in. None would even feed him when he begged for an apple or a crust of bread. That McMurdie had reported the theft of a peach by a starving boy to a man he knew damn well was violent with his child said everything Jeremy Trask needed to know about Baton Ridge. He was worth nothing to neither them nor his pa and he didn't know whether surviving another night of stark terror would come as a curse or a blessing.

Another fist. Jeremy's senses wavered; blackness gathered at the edges of his mind. He wished that blackness would swallow him, rescue him from the pain he knew was to come, but he wouldn't be that lucky. If his old man had beaten one thing into him it was toughness. He wouldn't black out because he could take the blows of a drunk and still remain conscious to suffer the after effects.

More blood in his mouth. The gunmetal taste sickened him but he dared not throw up. That would make things worse. Much worse.

'Please, Pa, I won't do it again.' Blood dribbled out as he spoke and it was as if it somehow inflamed the old man like a wolf drawing blood on a challenge to his dominion over the pack.

He laughed and Jeremy flinched with the burst of rancid breath tainted with whiskey and decay that assailed his nostrils.

'You steal once, boy, you never stop. I aim to make sure you never get the notion to try it again.'

'Would you rather I starved, you stupid old bastard?' he suddenly screamed, some burst of courage coming from a hidden place inside he hadn't known existed.

A mistake. A terrible mistake. One he regretted instantly.

A half-hour later, he huddled in a corner, bleeding from his mouth and nose and ears, paining in more places than he ever suspected he could hurt. He drew his legs up to his chest, and great sobs racked his body, each causing spikes of pain to radiate through his small battered form.

'You best learn your lesson, boy,' Jacob Trask said, hovering over him like some sort of drunken demon, knuckles smeared with his son's blood as well as his own. 'You ever talk to me that way 'gain you won't be gettin' up ever, you hear?'

Jeremy tried to nod, but it sent welts of pain through his neck and skull. Maybe he had gotten lucky, he thought, maybe this time the old man had really done some damage and broken something that would mean the death of his son. Maybe then the pain, the fear, the hopelessness would end.

But it hadn't ended, had it? He had

lived another day, another week, another year, each filled with the promise of harsher beatings.

Jeremy Trask came from his dark memories to find himself staring out the window of the mining shack, all the rage and pain and even terror he'd felt that day so long ago as fresh as it was the moment it happened. Days of pain, each running into the next, till they became a blur of never-ending torment. Until he'd finally gotten the balls to run away and learn to survive by robbing banks and stages and taking whatever he wanted. All the while gathering his courage to go back someday to that bastard town of Baton Ridge for a final confrontation with his father.

The very thing he had planned and James Darrow managed to prevent that day one year ago when the manhunter arrested him for bank robbery.

He reckoned some of that was his own fault; he had waited too long to act. It was damned peculiar how fear dug its way into a man's soul like a splinter that festered. It should have been easy to put a bullet into his father's brain and be done with it that day, but it hadn't been. Fear had paralyzed him, as if he were suddenly a child again, and he'd wait a moment too long. The old man had gotten lucky that day, lucky Jim Darrow had stopped him *en route* to the old shack and arrested him.

Four days ago he'd been too late again, hadn't he? The old man had got smart after learning his son had come back to Baton Ridge a year ago. He'd figured out the reason his bastard offspring was there that day and realized how close death had come to his door. And he'd realized his son would escape and come back for him one day. Because the Trask men held to certain patterns, didn't they? Mean ones, predictable ones. It was too embedded in their nature and what had saved Jacob Trask once would mean the death of him in short order.

The shack door rattled open and

Decker stepped inside. Trask eyed him. 'We got a mission. Fetch Trompson and get the horses saddled.'

'Mission?' Decker asked.

Trask nodded. 'Aim to kill two birds with one stone. We'll be stopping at a telegraph office, then payin' Lockeville a visit.'

Confusion touched Decker's features. 'Lockeville? Why there? Darrow's gonna be lookin' for us everywhere, shouldn't we just — ?'

The smile that came to Trask's lips stopped Decker cold. 'I aim to let him find us in Lockeville.'

Worry replaced confusion on Decker's face. Worry that said he had the notion his leader had gone plumb loco. Decker apparently thought better of voicing any protest. Instead, he ducked his chin to the corner, where the girl, Trallie, sat on her unfurled bedroll, knees drawn up to her chest, arms locked about them, head down.

'What's she been sulkin' about for the last two days?' Decker asked.

Trask laughed. 'Reckon she's just adjustin' to needin' a man.'

Trallie's head came up, disgust and spite raging in her eyes, but she said nothing. Decker's brow cinched and he shook his head, then left the shack.

Trask focused on the girl, almost giddy with expectation. 'Go with them, Trallie. See to it our little union stays between us and think about it happenin' again and again till you're fixed.'

Her face washed crimson and balls of muscle stood out on either side of her jaw. Without a word, she rose, gaze never wavering from Jeremy Trask as she walked out into the late afternoon sunlight.

He could not trust her to watch his back anymore, he felt certain. She had a powerful hate for him and would take the first chance at revenge she got. Maybe he could use that to his advantage at some point.

★ ★ ★

'Who'd you send that telegraph to?' Decker asked, as he sat in the saddle next to Jeremy Trask on a bluff overlooking Lockeville. Trompson sat to Trask's left, gazing downward.

Trask cast him an annoyed glance. Evening painted his hard face in shadow, making him appear somehow demonic. The air, stagnant with the scent of spring wildflowers, something Trask detested, didn't help his attitude any.

'You'll find out when I'm goddamn ready to tell you. Don't worry, won't be long.' Trask gave his man a cocky smile that obviously didn't please Decker but the second was smart enough to keep any further comment to himself.

'OK, then why are we here?' Decker asked instead, ducking his chin towards the town.

'We're here to visit my pa.' Trask uttered a lifeless chuckle.

'Your pa?' Trompson asked, his face pinching with confusion.

Trask nodded, gaze sweeping back to

the shadow-shrouded helltown below. 'I owe him something. Was aimin' to give it to him that day in Baton Ridge when Darrow found me. Was going to do the same thing when we rode in a few days ago. But the old sonofabitch musta smelled dung on the wind. He'd know I'd come for him someday.'

'How you know he's down there?' Decker asked.

'Trask brood's driven by habit, Decker. Fifth of the month; old bastard always heads here on the fifth of the month for a whore. Said Lockeville's got the best.'

'If he left Baton Ridge a 'cause he was scart of you coming back on him,' Trompson said, 'what makes you think he wouldn't avoid this place, habit or not?'

Trask's smile became poison. 'Because he can't, Trompson. He can't anymore than I could stop myself from making whoever wrongs me pay for it. Anymore than I could get the notion of butchering that whole goddamn town outa my mind that whole year I was in jail. Reckon you wouldn't expect to help a rattle-snake and not have it bite ya just the same . . . my pa's no different. I'm no different. He reckons he's safe for a day or two, reckons I wouldn't think he'd come here, and I'm bettin' he don't know yet I escaped, or about what happened in Baton Ridge. He'll be here, assuming he hasn't gone and got himself buried.'

Decker's brow knotted. 'What if he has?'

'That would be a goddamn shame,' Trask said, voice lowering as he saw a rider approaching from town. 'That would be a goddamn shame.'

Moments later, the rider drew up beside him. Trask duly noted the spite still in Trallie Hick's eyes. He would have figured she'd have gotten over it by now, but maybe that sickness she had was deeper than he had thought.

'You gonna let us know what you found or just sit there giving me the snake eyes?' Trask asked, when she didn't volunteer anything.

Her expression didn't change; it still said, 'I hate you, you sonofabitch. I hate you and I will never stop hating you until I find a way to get even.' He almost laughed.

'Marshal's in the saloon. He's half lubricated. Shouldn't be a problem.'

Trask studied her, uncertain from her tone whether she was lying. 'You best be tellin' me the truth, Trallie. Won't be merciful if you ain't.'

'I'm tellin' the truth.' Her words came with an unspoken: 'this time' attached. This time she was tellin' the truth, but there would come a time when that would not be the case, a time where it would be to her advantage and his death. He debated putting a bullet in her right then and there, but decided against it because he needed her for the moment.

'Let's go, then.' He slapped his heels into his stolen mount's flanks, sending it towards Lockeville.

Lockeville was an outhouse of a

town, rife with debauchery and sin for sale. Games of chance, women of pleasure, and shifty law that allowed owlhoots a stop-over free from harassment. Rowdy cowboys and vicious outlaw alike consorted here, calling an uneasy truce to sample life's baser pleasures, then rode off to face whatever came with their lot another day. Lawmen avoided Lockeville, except for its own marshal, a fella with his hand in as many tills as available and known for back-shooting those who complained or got on his bad side.

As they pulled up outside the saloon, Trask noted few folks wandered the street. He spotted a drunk pissing over a rail and two whores pleasuring fellas against buildings. Most reveled within the drinkerie, he reckoned, and he had counted on that. He was as vicious an outlaw as any who had ever come to this town to put on the elephant, but he was walking into a no-man's land of vice. This wasn't Baton Ridge; this wasn't easy pickin's:

he had to be prepared.

He reined up, dismounted, then tethered his horse to the hitch rail. Pausing, he noted the town smelled like piss, old liquor and dung, a blend of odors he despised solely because his old man had loved it.

He stepped on to the boardwalk, paused before the batwings. Jacob Trask was in there, somewhere. He could damn well feel him.

No, Pa, don't hit me anymore . . . please . . . I won't do it again, I swear I won't, I swear —

A measure of old fear trickled into his veins. He took a sharp breath. 'Not this time, old man,' he whispered. 'This time you'll know what it's like to be afraid of something so powerful you can't fight it. You'll goddamn know what I felt like all those years you beat the hell out of me.'

He turned back to his gang. 'Decker, wait outside. No one comes out of this saloon and lives to tell the tale, *comprende?*'

Decker, stepping on to the boardwalk along with Trallie and Trompson, nodded.

Trask turned, took a deep breath, then pushed through the batwings. Trallie and Trompson followed him in.

Standing on the landing overlooking the saloon proper, he surveyed the barroom, disappointment sinking in his belly.

Cowboys and owlhoots alike filled the place, some too drunk to lift their heads off the table, others too involved in chuck-a-luck, or faro, or poker to pay him notice. A couple of the outlaws appeared a little more wary, on guard in case some foolish lawdog decided he was tired of living and tried to take them in a snake's den such as this. Whores, their bosoms spilling from sateen bodices, mingled, hanging over the shoulders of winners, whispering sinful promises into their ears.

But of his father he saw no sign, and a peculiar relief mixed with disappointment washed through him. Old fears died hard.

One thing he noted: Trallie *had* been telling the truth this time. The marshal was indeed partially lubricated and laughing it up mightily at a poker table. A whore hung over him, rubbing her cleavage against the side of his bearded face.

A cruel smile filtered on to Trask's lips. He drew his Smith & Wesson, then took the three steps down to the saloon proper. He hoisted his gun and fired into the ceiling. The shot bellowed like thunder and discharged a cloud of blue smoke.

The saloon went dead silent. The piano player stopped playing; cowboys' mouths clamped shut; whores ceased giggling. Some of the outlaws looked ready to go for their guns.

As the marshal came half out of his chair, the whore at his shoulder slinked backwards, out of trouble's way.

Behind Trask, Trallie and Trompson whipped guns from holsters and aimed at the room.

'Now that I got your attention, my

name's Jeremy Trask. Reckon y'all heard a bit about me? If you ain't yet, you will. Any owlhoots in here, I ain't a threat to you, assumin' you don't do nothin' stupid. I come for Jacob Trask. I 'spect one of you knows where he might be.'

'Now see here,' the marshal said, fright on his face, but a certain drunken courage fueling his words. 'This is a safe town. You just can't come in here and — '

Trask swung his gun to the marshal. 'I ain't come for you, Marshal. Get out or die.'

The lawdog's courage evaporated with the stare Trask gave him. He nodded and scurried from his table to the batwings, passing between Trallie and Trompson, who made no move to stop him.

Trask waited a moment after the lawdog left. The crash of a gunshot came from outside. He smiled.

'That shot you just heard was the sound of your marshal meetin' his

Maker. Two things you best learn about me: I don't spare lawdogs and I don't ask questions twice.'

'Goddammit, you'll spoil things for all of us!' an owlhoot shouted, jumping from his chair, hand whisking for his gun.

Trask triggered a shot without an instant's hesitation. The owlhoot jumped backward as lead punched through his chest. He landed in a cloud of sawdust, lay still, blood pooling beneath him.

'Anyone else care to try their luck?' Trask asked.

'He's upstairs,' one of the owlhoots said, pointing to a staircase at the back of the room that led to an upper level where whores plied their trade.

Trask chuckled, a wave of relief washing over him. He had judged the old man right and this time Jacob Trask's cravings would be the death of him.

'Obliged.' Trask tipped the gun barrel to his hat brim. 'My two men will stay down here and keep you company while I go up and visit my pa. All goes well, you can go back to what you were doing — with a distraction or two — after about fifteen minutes.'

He walked to the back of the barroom, every gaze in the place following his path.

Hand on a banister, Trask peered at the landing above that led to a hallway lined with rooms. He forced away the last bit of fear and glanced at the Smith & Wesson in his other hand, a cruel smile back on his lips. 'Time's come, old man . . . '

He took the stairs slowly, each bootfall like the sound of thunder in his ears. Years, he'd waited, and now it came down to a single moment.

It dawned on him when he reached the top he'd neglected to ask for a room number but a moment later, when he entered a hallway, he discovered it didn't matter. Only one door of the six that lined either side was closed. The rest of the whores were still downstairs looking for marks. The night was still young.

Low-turned wall lantern light reflected off the red-striped foil wallpaper. A threadbare carpet covered the floor, muffling his bootfalls as he walked towards the closed door at the end of the hall.

His hand began to sweat around the gunbutt, something that never happened to him, and his heart picked up a step, beating a throbbing dirge.

Funny, indeed, how the past never truly stopped haunting a man.

When he reached the door, he drew a breath and slammed a foot against the panel. The door bounded inward, latch shattering, wood about it splintering.

'Well, well . . . ' he muttered, stopping in the doorway and peering in at the two occupants of the room. 'Reckon this fine establishment forgot to tell ya room service comes with lead.'

A young woman, naked, grabbed the dirty sheet to her chin, covering herself, and the older man in bed next to her, clad only in underwear, froze where he lay. Trask saw it in the old man's eyes that he recognized his bastard son and that death had come calling.

'You . . . ' Trask said, ducking his chin at the girl while keeping his gaze riveted on his father, 'get the hell out.'

'But I'm nekkid — ' the girl started, fear on her face.

Trask swung the Smith & Wesson towards the bardove. 'Like I told the folks below, I ain't one to ask a question twice.'

The girl's eyes flashed with the knowledge she could either be embarrassed by her nakedness or stop breathing. She jumped from the bed, grabbing her peek-a-boo blouse and skirt from a chair as she darted past him out into the hallway. He gave her a moment to get downstairs, heard a stifled whistle he guessed could only have come from Trallie and knew the dove had done as she was told. He hoped Trallie didn't get any fool notions because a naked gal had been put in front of her.

'Whatcha want, Jeremy?' his father asked, still frozen.

Trask came into the room, then eased the door shut behind him. It hung open an inch since his kick had destroyed the latch.

'You know damn well what I want, old man. I see it in your eyes.'

Terror spread over his father's face and Jeremy Trask felt any remains of his own fear die permanently. This was everything he had waited for, dreamed about. His father at *his* mercy.

Jacob Trask came from his spell and crawled from the bed, getting on his hands and knees on the floor before his son's feet. The older man shook, likely as much from years of drinking as from fear.

'Please, son, I'm sorry for all I done to you. I should never have done it.'

Trask let out a laugh he hadn't intended. How tragically weak and shattered the old man looked now. Was this the monster who'd tortured him all those years? Was this the man who instilled so much terror and turned his own son into the brutal beast he had grown to be? Maybe the Devil did have a sense of humor.

'Would you be sayin' the same if I didn't have a gun on you, Pa? Did you ever think that way when you were pounding the goddamn horsecrap outa me when I couldn't defend myself? Things have changed, you sonofabitch. I'm you, now. You taught me how to shut off my feelings, how to destroy those weaker then me. You taught me how to instill fear and treat life like the piece of dirt it is. You taught me goddamn well.'

Trask shot his father in the leg. The old man let out a strangled bleat and grabbed at the wound. Blood streamed between his fingers and saliva snaked from the corner of his mouth.

'God, no, please, don't kill me, boy. I'm powerful sorry. I truly am . . .'

Trask shot him in the other leg. Jacob Trask let out a screech this time, the pain and fright unhinging him. 'Oh, Jesus!' he shouted. 'Oh, Christ Jesus, you can't do this, you can't do this!'

'You suddenly gone an' got religion, Pa?' Trask uttered another laugh, this one filled with spite and disgust. 'Christ, you're just a goddamn coward at heart, ain't you? All those years you thought you were strong 'cause you beat me, all those years you told me I was the yellow-belly. But it wasn't me, was it? It was you. You were too goddamned small to face yourself.'

A defiant spark came into the elder Trask's eyes. 'I provided for you, you bastard. You know I did. I gave you shelter and made you tough enough for that goddamn town.'

Jeremy Trask knelt, one forearm draped over his left knee, the gun hanging relaxed in the other hand. 'I'll give you that much, old man. You made me into something other folk will tremble at with the mention of my name. But I don't know if I can rightly thank you for it.'

The old man's eyes filled with tears, which streamed down his face. 'Please, you can't do this . . . you can't . . . I don't want to die . . . '

Trask's eyes narrowed, his nostrils pinching with a whiff of the old man's whiskey- and rot-glazed breath. How he recollected that odor, how it brought dark memories back to him. 'At least have the balls to die like man, you no-good prick.'

Trask jerked the gun up and jammed the barrel to his father's forehead. He pulled the trigger a fraction later.

It took him a few minutes to get his hearing back after the thunder of that shot. Time seemed to stop and Jeremy Trask, staring down at his father's corpse, reckoned he should have felt more satisfied now that it was over, but something rang hollow about the victory, something oddly . . . sad.

'What the hell . . . ?' he muttered, forcing the feeling down, then leaving the room.

He came down the stairs slowly,

everyone in the barroom watching him, even Trallie and Trompson from the landing.

'Reckon I'm finished here,' he said to them when he took the three steps to the landing and stopped beside them. 'Trallie, you're comin' with me. Can't trust you around bar gals. Fact, can't trust you period. Send Decker in here.'

She cast him a look but turned and went through the batwings.

'Why are we stayin' behind?' Trompson asked, a measure of doubt in his voice.

'Think I told you I aim to kill two birds with one stone: you'll be takin' care of the second bird.'

5

'Why would Trask, assuming it was him, wipe out a whole town?' Marshal Dan Mason asked, as late afternoon clogged the corners of his office with gray shadows. He sat with his feet up on his desk, a puzzled look on his young face.

Jim Darrow stood by the window, gazing out at the waning day. Spring Treller sat in a hardbacked chair in front of the desk, her arms wrapped about herself, face tight. Despite the anxiety riding his nerves, Jim couldn't help noticing how lovely she looked now that her bruises and swelling had started to fade and a couple of days' worth of square meals had filled out her features. Her eyes carried a sparkle that might have been hope, or maybe she was just focused now. Whatever it was, it was better than the desperate defeat and surrender he had seen in them two days ago.

They'd spent those past two days finding exactly no leads to Jeremy Trask or his men, and that was starting to frustrate the hell out of him. He had to admit he was rusty after a year away from manhunting, but the fact that nobody had seen Trask meant either the outlaw was lying low or had pulled stakes. If the outlaw made it to Mexico, they might never find him. But something inside, the same thing that told him Trask had killed Clay, told him the sonofabitch was still somewhere close, that he hadn't finished with his plan of blood.

'Jim?' Mason asked, pulling him from his thoughts.

'Yeah?' he mumbled, turning to face the lawman.

'You're a million miles away.' Mason slid his feet off the desk and leaned forward.

'Reckon I'm just frustrated we haven't gotten a lead.'

'He might be gone.'

'He's not gone.' Jim frowned. 'I feel him out there. He butchered that town for a reason.'

'All due respect to that manhunter's sixth sense, you might just be holdin' to a hope you can catch up to him and kill him for Clay's death. Most outlaws would be smart enough to head to Mex or some place they ain't likely to be followed or caught by the law.'

'Maybe . . . ' He shrugged, knowing rationally Mason made perfect sense, but he couldn't shake the feeling Trask had more than just killing a town in mind. 'That day I went to Baton Ridge to bring him back for trial, I got the notion he'd gone there to take care of some unfinished business.'

'How tell?' Mason jammed his elbows on the desk top and Spring's gaze followed Jim intently.

'When I cornered him he was surprised. Reckon part of that came from the fact his own town had turned him in — he as much as said so. But his first words were 'No, not yet . . . ' Didn't really strike me as anything meaningful at the time, but now I gotta wonder if there wasn't something he wanted in Baton Ridge. Maybe that's why he butchered that town. But whatever it was, I'm wonderin' if he found it. If he didn't, he might hang close until he does.'

'All due respect, you got nothin' to base that on, Jim. You were one of the best manhunters in the territory, but you ain't been in the saddle for a year. We don't even know for sure he butchered that town. Only witness didn't see who did it.' Mason cast Spring a glance and she kept silent.

'He did it.' Jim's tone came hard, certain.

Mason shrugged. 'I'm inclined to agree, but we might have a matter of proving it even if we do bring him in.'

Coldness washed across Jim's eyes. 'I'm not plannin' on bringin' him in this time.'

Mason nodded, face going somber.

He realized what Jim meant and wasn't inclined to argue the case, since his own friend had been killed directly after Trask's escape. Jim wondered if Mason would turn the other way if Trask ended up hanging from a cottonwood, but he'd deal with that when the time came.

'I saw one of his gang,' Spring said, breaking the tension. 'I'll testify to it.'

Jim peered at her, seeing the same look of vengeance in her eyes as he felt in his heart. She wanted the outlaw who had raped her dead, not behind bars.

Dan Mason sighed heavily. 'OK, so we just wait around till he gets cocky and makes a mistake?'

Jim shook his head. 'Trask didn't strike me as the cocky type.'

'How'd he strike you?' Spring asked, her voice low.

'He struck me as the determined type, single-minded. He knew he was wanted for that robbery a year ago. The men wore masks but he got stupid and pulled his down right as he reached the edge of town. Lady saw him from a window and pointed him out in court. Only thing that got him convicted, if not for murder . . . ' Jim's words trailed off and he paused, the pain of losing Clay sending an acute ache through his belly. 'He just didn't expect that town to give him up and for me to arrive quite so soon.'

'He should have . . . from what I've heard about Baton Ridge they don't do anything unless it's to save their own asses. They only turned him in because they didn't want trouble for themselves. They got no loyalty to their own.'

Jim nodded. 'You can ask Spring about that. They would have let her die rather than feed her. Hell, maybe they got what they deserved.' With the thought of what might have happened to the young woman bitterness swelled within him. The feeling surprised him, even made him a bit ashamed at what he'd said, but he couldn't stop it. He'd spent a lot of time with her over the past couple days, maybe too much.

'Jim,' Mason said, frowning. 'You know you don't mean that, no matter how cold those folks were. If Trask did this he's a goddamned monster.'

Jim nodded. 'Beg your pardon, Dan. You're right. And you'll get no argument from me on Trask being a monster.'

Mason gave him a reassuring smile. 'Reckon I won't hold it against you. We're all a bit testy after what happened. Still don't make a lot of sense, though. What could possibly be so important he would risk being brought in? And why would he hate a town enough to butcher everyone in it, even if they did turn him in? He went up for robbery, had maybe two more years to go on his term. Mass murder is a whole different horse.'

'There had to be somethin' there he wanted, maybe even someone he hated. And maybe that hate meant more to him than his freedom. Like I said, he gave me the notion of a man determined, but maybe it went deeper than that. Maybe he's a man driven by things he can't control.'

'But the town?' Mason asked.

'Spring said they never did anything for their own. Maybe he held a grudge against them that went deeper than just their turning him over to the law.'

Paleness washed across Mason's face. 'A grudge powerful enough to do what he did to all those innocent people?'

'Hate's a peculiar thing, Dan. You let it live in you long enough it takes over, corrupts your soul. I gotta reckon if he went back to kill someone in that town a year ago, his hate only grew while he sat in that cell. It grew from something evil already inside him.'

'Still seems extreme, don't it?' Mason said, as if wanting to deny a human being could be that vicious.

'To most of us, but to Trask?' Jim shrugged. 'Who knows? But make no mistake about it, that man was a killer long before he rode into Baton Ridge four days ago and after you've killed one it ain't such a big step to killing many. The numbers get blurred and pretty soon you forget the faces.'

'Sounds like you're talkin' from experience,' Spring said in a distressed tone.

Jim nodded. 'I ain't proud of the fact I've had to kill men in my job. Was necessary because if I hadn't they would have killed me. But I still see every face in my nightmares and I still feel guilt over it.'

'Will you feel guilt after you kill Trask?' she asked, her gaze locking with his and he couldn't tell whether it was accusation or sympathy in her eyes.

He turned away, swallowing hard and peering at nothing in particular out in the street.

Dan Mason leaned back and pulled open a drawer, bringing out a file folder and tossing it atop his desk. He closed the drawer, then opened the file, sifted through a number of the papers.

'Not a lot on Trask I could find,' the marshal said. 'Seems he got into a number of scrapes as a young man, but nothing major got pinned on him till the robbery.'

'Just because he wasn't caught doesn't mean he wasn't doin' the Devil's work,' Spring said, spite in her tone. 'If he's anything like . . . the one who raped me, he's poison.'

'Inclined to think he's worse,' Mason said.

'He got any kin he might hole up with?' Jim asked, turning back to Mason. Outside the sun had dropped behind the distant Rockies and the room had turned to sepia. Spring got up and went to a wall lantern, fired it, then returned to her chair.

'Says he has a father. Not much about how they got on, but his mother died under peculiar circumstances when Trask was a child. Apparently they tried to pin something on the father but the case was dismissed due to lack of evidence.'

'Apples don't fall far . . . ' Spring said.

'Where's the father now?' Jim asked.

Mason shrugged, then ran a hand through his prematurely graying hair. 'No idea. Apparently he left town right before the trial and hasn't been heard from since.'

'That doesn't help us much.' A note of anxiety hung in Spring's voice. With it, she tensed, and Jim reckoned she was thinking about what Trask's man had done to her. She was tired of waiting for vengeance and Jim couldn't blame her. The same anxious frustration ran through his own veins.

'No, it don't.' Mason slapped the folder shut. 'Question is, what's our next step?'

Jim frowned. 'Can't see one unless he strikes again or someone spots him. No chance of tracking him out of Baton Ridge. Too many tracks leading every which direction and we got no idea what they were riding for horses.'

The door rattled open and a boy who

couldn't have been more than sixteen bounded in, a slip of yellow paper in his hand.

'Got a telegram for Mr. Darrow,' said the boy, coming up to Jim and holding out the paper. 'Mr. Becker said I should bring it right away a'cause of what it said.'

Jim took the paper, fished a coin from his pocket, then handed it to the boy. After the boy left, Jim glanced at the note. A dark look crept across his face and a wave of coldness swarmed through his innards.

'What is it?' Spring asked, rising from her chair. He looked over at her, saw what actually looked like concern in her eyes, and for an instant it melted some of the ice in his belly. He walked to the desk and passed the telegram to Mason.

' 'You want Jacob Trask',' Mason read aloud, ' 'Come to Lockeville and bring the girl, stop. Eight tonight.' Ain't signed.'

'Who's Jacob Trask?' Spring asked.

Mason flipped the folder back open, eyes roving a moment. 'That's the old man's name.'

'That begs two questions, don't it?' Jim said. 'One, how would anyone know we were even thinking about looking for Trask's father and, two, why would someone give him to us on a platter?'

'A trap . . . ' Mason said, frowning.

Jim nodded. 'Sounds like, because I'm bettin' it's plain who that telegram came from.'

'Jeremy Trask,' Mason said.

Spring peered at Johnny. 'What was that you were sayin' about him not bein' the cocky sort?'

He shook his head. 'Not cocky, calculating. My guess is someone saw us in Baton Ridge and reported back to Trask. If he wasn't stickin' around at that point, he is now, because he knows I'll be after him and he figures you'll be able to identify his man and link him to the butchering of Baton Ridge. With you dead, he goes back to jail for robbery and escape; with you alive, he gets a necktie party.'

'Reckon he's smart enough to know he gets his either way with you on his tail,' Mason said. 'And I reckon he's smart enough to know we'd be lookin' for any connection to him and his pa would show up as the only one. Figures he would make good bait.'

'You think his pa's really in that town?' Spring asked.

Jim shrugged. 'Hard to say. What ain't hard to say is he wants me there.'

'He wants us both there.' An almost eager light dawned in Spring's eyes.

'Which is why you're stayin' here.' Johnny said, the peculiar protective feeling welling in him again.

'You mean you're just going to ride into a trap?' Mason asked, surprise hanging in his tone.

Johnny nodded. 'Aim to. We got no other leads. Can you think of a better way to find one?'

Mason's brow cinched. 'I can think of better ways to stay amongst the living.'

'I ain't askin' you to come, Dan. Let me go alone. I need someone here to protect Spring in case things don't work out.'

'I don't need protectin'!' Spring said, face reddening. 'Trask's *man* made me do . . . well, I aim to settle that score myself.'

'It's too dangerous,' Jim said, tone determined. 'You'll stay here.'

She gave him a scoffing laugh. 'I reckon it isn't half as dangerous as being caught in that town the day he rode in. I can't live with knowin' those sonsofbitches are out there, maybe doing to someone else what they did to me, and not liftin' a finger to prevent it. You can't stop me. I'll just follow you, so I reckon it's best you take me with.'

'I'll be goin' too, Jim,' Mason said. 'He or one of his gang likely killed a friend of mine and I ain't about to lose another by letting you charge in after him alone.'

Jim nodded, deciding he had no time to argue them out of it. 'Lockeville's a half-hour from here. It's seven-fifteen now. We barely got time to saddle up and head out.'

'Reckon Trask planned it that way,' Spring said, already heading for the door.

'Reckon he's planned a lot of things,' Jim said, starting after her.

'None of 'em good,' Mason added, following suit.

*   *   *

Night had fallen by the time they reached Lockeville and reined to a halt on the bluff overlooking the town. Jim Darrow peered down, surveying the wide main street, eyes narrowing.

'Awful quiet, ain't it?' Mason said beside him, leaning forward, bracing a forearm on the saddle horn. 'This town's usually hell on hoofs.'

Jim nodded. 'Hear tell there's an unwritten law that makes it a sanctuary for cowboy and outlaw alike. Law never goes in there after owlhoots. They did, they'd never come back out.'

'You ever consider chasing a man there?' Mason peered at him, eyes hard.

He shook his head. 'Too dangerous. Never know who or how many's gonna backshoot you. Was always better to wait until your quarry got himself lubricated and headed out.'

Spring frowned. 'And now you got a notion to go in there alone after Trask? You got yourself a death-wish?'

He glanced at her, seeing concern in her eyes. 'Wish I knew what kinda wish I had . . . ' The words came dark and unbidden. Maybe he did have a deathwish. All he knew is some days he just wanted to stop the grief within him in any way possible, whether it meant taking a bullet himself, or putting one in the source of his misery — Jeremy Trask.

'Won't go away, you know,' Spring's voice softened.

'What won't?' Jim's brow cinched.

'The pain. Doesn't matter if you kill Trask, the pain will still be there.

Sooner or later you'll have to face it and let it go.'

'That what you plan on doing with the man who raped you?' He instantly regretted the harsh edge in his tone and felt like an ass, but her words pricked at him for a reason he couldn't pinpoint.

Her face tightened and sorrow bled from her eyes, but she ignored the cutting remark. 'I've lived with pain long enough to know there aren't any easy fixes. You think you got the answer, you think killing this man will stop you from hurting, but it won't. You best prepare yourself for that after you kill him . . . if he don't kill you.'

'This ain't the time to be gettin' ahead of ourselves,' Mason said, his voice low. 'Trask aims to kill you, Jim, or he wouldn't have sent that telegram. You best focus on that and save the philosophical talk for later.'

Mason was right but Jim still struggled with a measure of irritation; he hoped it wasn't because he suspected the young woman beside him might be right and he was simply too mule-headed to admit it.

'We're goin' down,' Jim said to Spring. 'You stay here. He wants you dead too and if we don't come back at least you got a shot at saving yourself and getting to the county marshal to tell him what happened.'

'I want to go with you. I want the one who raped me.'

He peered at her, searching her eyes, which were hard and reflecting vengeance. 'Will that end *your* pain?'

Pinching her lips shut, she said nothing. After a strained moment Jim turned to Mason and nodded. They gigged their mounts into a slow walk, maneuvering down the hillside. Spring stayed behind, an unreadable look in her eyes. Jim found himself unable to force her words out of his mind and he didn't need that right now. Too much was at stake — namely, his life and the life of the man next to him, as well as hers.

Mason glanced at Jim, his face

somber. 'She's startin' to have feelin's for you, you know that, don't you?'

'Like you said, now ain't the time for such talk.'

Mason uttered a strained laugh. 'You always were one good at avoidin' the obvious, Jim, my boy.'

'Reckon I heard enough from her already. Don't need you analyzing me, too.'

Mason's laugh came easier this time. 'Well, one last piece of analyzin', then: you're startin' to have feelin's for her, too.'

'The hell I am!' he said, too fast and with a bit too much denial.

'You're only foolin' yourself if you think I ain't right. I've seen the way you've been spending the past two days with her when you weren't searching for leads. You buy her meals, take care of her more like she was a wife than some girl you just pulled out of a bad situation. You reckon love at first sight exists, Jim?'

'Shut the hell up, Mason. We got a

job to do.' He tried to sound angry but didn't quite pull it off.

Mason uttered another soft laugh. 'Reckon you just answered my question, but I also reckon it's time to focus on Trask. That town's too damn quiet.'

Jim nodded as they reached the main street. Boardwalks were deserted, something highly unusual for Lockeville, and no sound came from anywhere. No clanking of a piano from the saloon, no bawdy laughter or shouts, curses or whoops. Nothing.

'That telegram didn't really tell us where to look, just to come here,' Mason said.

'I got a notion we try the saloon. Should be sounds coming from it, but I don't hear anything. Reckon that makes it best the place to start.'

'Or to die . . . ' Mason's tone darkened.

Jim nodded. 'Or to die.'

They headed to the saloon, Jim slipping from the saddle before his horse even came to a stop. Mason followed suit and they guided their horses to the hitch rail and tethered the reins.

Jim ducked his chin to a body lying on the boardwalk in front of the batwings and Mason nodded, drawing his gun. They went to the corpse and Jim knelt, felt for a pulse. He glanced up at Mason, shook his head.

'The marshal . . . ' Dan Mason said.

Jim straightened. 'Trask's work, I reckon.'

Mason nodded. 'We'd best be prepared for worse, then, if Baton Ridge was any marker.'

Jim's hand went to the Peacemaker at his hip, slid it from its holster. He frowned, then moved towards the batwings.

'Take my back.' Jim lifted the gun to his cheek and Mason nodded.

With a deep breath, Jim pushed through the batwings, Mason a step behind. He halted on the landing almost instantly, surveying a sea of tense faces about the barroom, fear in the eyes of cowboy and outlaw alike. No one said a word, no one moved.

'What the hell — ?' he started, then heard the *skritch* of a hammer drawing back.

'Be obliged if you'd both set your guns down slowly,' came a voice behind him to his left. Jim glanced back, both ways, noting a man pressed to the wall to either side of the batwings. Both held guns on him and Mason. He recognized neither, but pegged them as Trask's men.

'Where's Trask?' Jim asked, not making a move to comply with the man's order.

One of the men, the taller one to his left, uttered a harsh laugh. 'Oh, he sends his regards . . . and his condolences on your brother's death.'

Fury sizzled through Jim's veins at the mention of his brother and he half considered swinging and trying to take down the man who had said it. But could he count on Mason guessing his move and swinging on the other man in time to prevent one of them from dying on the spot?

'Now, put your guns down,' the taller man said, 'then walk down them steps in front of you.'

Jim spotted a pile of firearms off to the left, one he'd never reach, even if it might have done him any good. He reckoned they must have collected the weapons from everyone in the place. He also noticed another body, an outlaw, possibly, lying on the barroom floor. That told him this was not only going to mean death for him and Mason, but likely another whole-sale slaughter that would leave no witnesses to point the way to Trask. After that it likely wouldn't take them long to track down Spring and kill her too.

He saw no choice. They were going to die but he would go down fighting. He only hoped Mason had an inkling of what he intended to do. Without another thought, he swung on the taller man.

Damn him! Spring Treller thought as she watched Jim Darrow and Dan Mason ride towards the town. Jim had no right telling her she couldn't come with them. Those men had murdered her whole town and that gal . . .

She had been too ashamed to tell Jim Darrow that the one who defiled her was a woman. Maybe it didn't matter because rape was rape and that was hard enough to admit, but would the fact it had been a woman make him think different of her, make her even more soiled than she was already? Would it destroy any chance she had of him . . .

Loving you?

She had no call even thinking that way, but how he saw her suddenly mattered to her, more than it should have.

She shook off the thoughts, focusing instead on the woman who had violated her and rage flowed through her veins.

What are you going to do when you find her?

She asked herself that for the hundredth time in the past two days. Kill her, the way Jim intended to kill Trask? When it came down to facing that gal, could she pull the trigger? Lord knew she wanted to, had envisioned that gal's body lying at her feet full of holes. But even with all the hate seething inside her, she was no cold-blooded killer, despite the fact she had tried to shoot Jim in Baton Ridge. Then, she had been half-mad with hunger and rage and defeat. But now that she had gotten time to think, had shelter and food . . .

But would bringing in the woman do any good? Would any court convict her for such a deed? Spring knew the way such things were treated out here. There were times a woman was no more than property in this man's West, so what chance would she have in a room full of men? Maybe there was no such thing as justice for a woman named Spring Treller. Maybe what had begun in Baton Ridge was a locked trail of fate and she could do nothing more than surrender to the inevitable.

And maybe a man like Jim Darrow, assuming he survived whatever trap Trask had laid for him in Lockeville, only felt sorry for her and would be so repulsed by what had happened with Trask's gal he would never be able to fall in love with her.

The thought knotted emotion in her throat.

She bit her lower lip against the confusion swimming in her mind. She told herself she was overreacting, but maybe the small hope Jim Darrow had given her was nothing more than a dream, a bird without wings.

She'd never get the chance to find out, though, would she, if he got himself killed down in that town? She knew what Trask and his gang were capable of. But in Baton Ridge they had the element of surprise and town indifference on their side. She reckoned that same element could be turned against them. Trask likely expected Jim and her to ride in, not Jim and Mason, leaving her behind. Trask also likely didn't expect a woman who could shoot as well as any man and one with a powerful hate fueling her actions.

Without another thought she gigged her horse into motion, sending it careening down the bluff. If she had learned anything over the past few months on her own, it was not to let your fate rest in another's hands. She was starting to trust Jim Darrow, but that didn't mean she would let him tell her what to do.

Besides, he had only told her to stay on the bluff; he'd neglected to tell her how long. She reckoned it had been long enough.

She slowed as she reached the town, jumped from her horse while it was still in motion. She had spotted Jim and Mason's mounts tethered to the rail outside the saloon, so she pulled her own horse in that direction. After tethering the animal, she eased on to the boardwalk, then stopped at the body of the dead lawman. She froze for an instant, a vision of the bloody bodies scattered about Baton Ridge flashing through her mind, overwhelming her with emotion.

'Be strong . . . ' she told herself. 'Jim and Mason are walking into a trap. Least you can do is hold up till you know they're all right . . . '

She forced herself to kneel and pull the lawman's gun from its holster.

She moved to the batwings, just as a shout came from within . . .

★ ★ ★

Jim's gun arced around and he drew a bead on the taller man standing a few feet to the left of the batwings.

Shock swept across the man's face; he wasn't quite prepared for the move and let out a shout, jerking his own gun forward. But surprise wouldn't matter, because the outlaw's gun was aimed

151

dead center of Jim's chest.

A heartbeat behind, Dan Mason swung his own gun, by some miracle picking up on what Jim intended and going the opposite way as if they choreographed the maneuver. The marshal's gun arced to the shorter man standing to the right.

Jim's shot would not come in time. He knew it, but had no time to whisper even a prayer to a God he had no faith would listen.

The thunder of a shot filled the barroom.

The taller man flew sideways, his gun discharging, bullet shrieking by Jim, missing by a hair. An orchid of blood appeared on the outlaw's chest as he tumbled off the landing and hit the floor hard in a cloud of sawdust. His Smith & Wesson landed a score of feet away, beneath a table. An outlaw grabbed it.

In a blink Jim saw the reason the man had missed his own shot and ended up writhing on the floor. Spring stood just inside the batwings, both hands clamped around a gun he reckoned she must have taken off the dead lawman on the boardwalk. Her face was nearly as bleached as her hands.

Another shot thundered and horror surged through him.

Marshal Dan Mason bounded backward off the landing, a bullet from the short man's gun punching through his chest. The shorter man had gotten his shot off a split second before Mason's spasming finger pulled the trigger on his own gun.

The marshal's bullet drilled into a wall. Mason landed in a cloud of sawdust that drizzled over him like death snow.

No time to dwell on it, Jim swung his gun as the shorter man tried to adjust his aim and fire at the manhunter.

Jim fired first. Lead slammed the outlaw backward into the wall beside the batwings, suspending him there as if by invisible strings. He coughed a spray of blood, then slid downward, eyes blank, gun dropping from his nerveless fingers. On his knees, he pitched face-first to the floor, lay still.

Jim whirled, his Peacemaker coming to aim on the outlaw who had grabbed the gun dropped by Trask's man. The owlhoot's eyes locked with Jim's, then he reversed the gun in his grip and handed it over.

'You'll get no trouble from any of us,' the outlaw said. 'You probably just saved all our asses.'

Jim nodded, jammed the gun into his belt then went to Mason.

He knelt, lifting the marshal's head. Blood trickled from the lawman's mouth and a dull film glazed his eyes.

'Oh, Christ, Dan, I'm sorry,' Jim whispered, his heart burning.

'I . . . I know, Jim. Find Trask . . . kill . . . kill him once for me, too . . . ' The marshal's head fell back and Jim set it gently on the floor. He passed a hand over the lawman's eyelids, closing them, then pressed his own lips together tight to stop them from quivering.

Goddammit, this wasn't how it was s'posed to go. The heroes always came out on top, didn't they? What the hell was wrong with this goddamn world? First Clay, now another good man . . . one he hadn't been able to save, either.

He came to his feet, glanced at Spring, who still stood just inside the doors, shaking.

'Is he . . . ?' she asked and Jim nodded.

'Reckon you saved my life,' he said. 'He'd be proud of you.'

'I . . . I never killed no one before.' A tear slid down her face. 'It feels horrible . . . '

His voice lowered. 'You had no choice. Either of these the man who raped you?'

She shook her head. 'No . . . '

'And Trask didn't bother sticking around. He must have had a lot of faith in these two.'

With a deep breath, she lowered the gun. 'They broke him out of jail and

155

took down a whole town. Reckon he had reason to.'

He glanced at the shorter of the two outlaws, determining the man was dead instantly. With a look at the second he saw the fellow was still alive, barely, groaning, his lifeblood forming a gory lake on the floorboards. Jim slid his Peacemaker into its holster, then went to the man.

The outlaw peered at him with dazed eyes as Jim knelt and grabbed two handfuls of the man's shirt.

'You'll get no mercy from me, you sonofabitch. A good man died here tonight and if I had my way I'd hand you over to the Devil personally.'

'Go to hell, Darrow.' The man spat, and saliva mixed with blood trickled down Jim's face. Rage burned within him, unbridled but impotent over the death of Mason.

He shook the outlaw, drew the man's face closer to his own. His words came through gritted teeth. 'I can make your last minutes so goddamn painful you'll scream for death, you bastard. Tell me where Trask is and I'll let you die peacefully.'

The man gazed at him, likely only half seeing him. He started to laugh, a maniacal defiant thing and Jim knew he'd get nothing from the outlaw.

A breath later, the man's head fell back and Jim slammed him to the floor in an uncontrollable burst of anger and frustration. Any lead to Trask had just perished.

He stood, a sea of stunned and not-a-little relieved faces riveted to him and the young woman still shaking in front of the batwings.

He peered at them, face hard, eyes dark.

'I need a buckboard and two men to take my friend out gently after hitching it to my horse. These other two' — he glanced at each of the fallen outlaws — 'you can feed 'em to the buzzards for all I give a damn . . .'

6

She'd killed a man. No matter how hard Spring tried to tell herself her actions had been justified, that if she hadn't shot him that outlaw would have killed Jim, she couldn't get the sight of that bullet punching into that man's chest out of her mind. The sound it made, the brittle cracking of bone; the blood swelling against his shirt; the terrible knowledge of one's own death that had flashed into his eyes . . . all those would live with her for the rest of her days.

As she walked along the boardwalk, the new morning somehow mockingly tranquil, sunlight sparkling from troughs and glinting from windows, the memory twisted in her belly. She went to a rail, leaned over, bile surging into her throat. She gulped deep breaths, struggling to hold on to her breakfast. After a few minutes, she managed to force some of the nausea away.

Killing, no matter how necessary, was different when you actually went through with the deed. Many times over the past few days had she imagined the look of death on the face of the gal who'd raped her, but it didn't compare to the real thing and she took no satisfaction in what she'd done. That man she had killed, he had likely murdered countless others in her town the day he rode in with Trask, but even that knowledge didn't erase the sick feeling she got thinking about how she had taken his life.

Or the thought she would do it again if she had to to protect Jim Darrow.

It was ironic, she reckoned. She had accompanied Jim and Dan Mason to Lockeville with the intent to kill the woman who had defiled her, but now, if that woman stood before her, she knew she could not take her life in cold blood.

She pushed herself away from the rail

and wandered along the boardwalk, legs a trifle unsteady. She tried to focus on the peacefulness of the morning, how the sun glazed the streets with gold and filled the place with a serene beauty she'd never witnessed in Baton Ridge.

She had reckoned every town to be the same, but maybe she had been wrong. Jim Darrow was certainly nothing like the men in Baton Ridge; he had been kind to her, offered her shelter and food without expecting anything in return. In fact, she had glimpsed something in his eyes last night when he wanted to prevent her from going with them to Lockeville — concern for her safety. He hadn't been just ordering her like she was some helpless woman incapable of anything but attending to her man's needs; he had wanted to protect her. And those feelings came from something deeper than an attempt at chivalry, they had come from —

'You're plumb loco!' she scolded herself. A man like that — what the hell would he want with a woman like her? A woman who hadn't even been able to keep herself off the streets, a woman forced to beg for help from strangers?

Coming from her thoughts she noticed a small white church across the street. Beside it sat a smaller building, also white, with a small picket fence and beds ablaze with spring flowers. She'd never seen anything like that in Baton Ridge. Nobody there had given a damn about flowers, and nobody had given a damn about new life and simple human dignity.

Outside the smaller house stood a woman, one with child, tending the flowers. Spring recognized her from the day she'd come in with Jim and seen him holding her in the street. She was the woman whose husband had been killed in Baton Ridge. Her face was haggard, burdened with a terrible sadness, one Spring recognized from experience. The loss of her husband was tearing her apart. She felt lost, alone, unsure of the future and frightened for the life of her unborn child.

Emotion swelled in Spring's throat as her own feelings of loss flooded back from the day they'd told her of her husband's death. But there was a difference, wasn't there? No one in Baton Ridge had offered her help that day or any day thereafter. No one had offered her even a kind word. This woman, she'd gotten all that Spring had desperately needed; she would be helped.

Spring scolded herself for the sudden burst of envy that rose in her mind. That wasn't her; she was happy for this woman, happy she would not be forced to endure the nights on the street and the hunger burning in her belly.

But pain was pain, grief was grief, and this woman was alone, with child. For all Spring had suffered, she reckoned she had only feared for her own life. This woman feared for two and that brought a deep sympathy and sadness to her soul.

Any flicker of envy vanished with that thought and the only thing left in her mind was helping that woman somehow, comforting her, letting her know that though she was by herself, she wasn't truly alone.

She stepped off the boardwalk and crossed the street. A passerby tipped his hat to her and a woman strolling by smiled warmly. Spring didn't quite know what to make of their kindness.

As she came up to the young pregnant woman a thin smile played on her lips and awkward feelings plagued her mind. This was foolish; what could she say to ease her pain? Words didn't make things better.

But feelings did. Feelings of companionship and empathy. Baton Ridge might have beaten everything else out of her, but not her compassion.

The young woman looked at her and Spring tried to smile. The young woman's eyes were red and puffy, with dark pouches beneath. The tracks of her tears still showed on her cheeks.

'Mornin',' the young woman said, her smile feeble as she returned the expression.

Spring nodded. 'My name's Spring. I was in Baton Ridge the day . . .' Dammit, that wasn't what she had meant to say. It had just been so long since she'd tried to comfort anyone she had trouble finding the right words.

The young woman nodded. 'I saw you ride in with Jim.' Her voice held a tremble, one summoned by grief.

'I was the only survivor.' She stared at the ground a moment, searching for something, anything that would ease some of this woman's pain, but coming up empty. Maybe this had been a bad idea.

'I'm Tessy,' the young woman said. 'My husband . . .'

Spring nodded. 'I know. Reckon that's why I came over. I lost my husband a while back, too. Thought maybe if you wanted to talk to someone who had been through the same thing . . .'

Tears started flowing from the young woman's eyes. 'Did you see . . . did you see who did it?'

Spring frowned, shook her head. 'I . . . no, one of the gang . . . one of them had me in an alley and — '

The young woman's tears came harder. 'I'm sorry, it must have been horrible for you.'

Spring tried to force the image of what happened in that alley from her mind. She wasn't here for herself: she was here for this woman. 'Like I said, I survived, but I want you to know I understand what you're going through, some of it anyway. If I can help . . . '

The young woman smiled a fragile smile. 'You're very kind. I reckon in a way I'm lucky; I got folks in this town willing to help. The ladies at the church, they said I could stay until I have the baby and then they'll make sure I got a place. The town . . . ' She sniffled, and Spring could tell she was overwhelmed with emotion. 'The town took up a collection for me.'

Spring nodded, a brief spike of envy stabbing her again, but she instantly repressed it.

'I'm glad for you, Tessy,' Spring said. 'I'm glad someone cares in this town. Baton Ridge wasn't that way.'

The young woman searched her eyes, the thin smile back. 'But you are that way, aren't you? You came over to me when you didn't even know me and offered a kind word and your help.'

Spring wrapped her arms about herself, brow knitting. 'Reckon someone's got to atone for that town's sins.'

'Looks like someone already did . . .' Her words came with sadness and spite and she shuddered.

'Jim knows who did it, Tessy. He'll bring the sonofabitch in.'

The young woman's face darkened with anger. 'I want that man dead. I ain't ashamed to admit it. I want him dead for what he did to my husband. He was a good man. He worked hard to provide and we were just startin' our life together.' Tessy broke down and

Spring took her in her arms. The young woman sobbed against her shoulder. 'I miss him, I miss him powerfully.'

'I know you do, Tessy,' Spring whispered. 'I know you do. Wish I could tell you you'll stop missin' him, but you won't. You just go on with your life. You got your memories of him. Hold on to that, Tessy. And tell your young un what a fine man he was.'

Tessy drew back, eyes red, searching. 'But the pain . . .'

Spring wiped a tear from Tessy's cheek, struggled not to choke up. 'It will ease some, Tessy. I promise. Not for a spell, but one day you'll wake up and smile when you think of him.'

'How can you say that after what you've been through? You were there when those men rode in and killed everyone.'

'I . . . I don't know. It's just who I am, I reckon. Maybe that makes me plumb loco or something.'

'No.' Tessy shook her head, hugged Spring again. 'That makes you special.'

167

It took the young woman ten minutes to stop crying and Spring held her all that time, rubbing her back, letting her bleed her sorrow.

'I best be goin' now,' Spring said, when Tessy at last got her composure back.

'Thank you for your kindness.' Tessy smiled, wiped tears from her face.

'You recollect what I said, you need someone to talk to . . .'

Tessy nodded and Spring turned away, taking a few steps, then stopping again. She looked back to Tessy.

'The man who brought me in, Jim Darrow, he's a good man, isn't he?'

Tessy nodded. 'One of the best. He ain't been himself since his brother was killed. Maybe you could help him find that again.'

'What do you mean?'

Tessy's smile was softer this time. 'There's a light in your eyes when you say his name.'

★   ★   ★

Jim Darrow stood in the marshal's office, sorrow and anger burning a hole in his belly. Shafts of amber light stabbed through the windows, falling over the empty chair behind the marshal's desk and making the room feel somehow haunted.

You knew it was a trap, Jim told himself as he peered at that chair. *You should have gone alone.*

'Goddammit!' he yelled, rage suddenly overwhelming him. He kicked the small table holding the coffee pot and sent it flying. The pot bounced from a wall and splattered leftover coffee across the floor.

A good man was dead because of that sonofabitch. Another good man. And an entire town and Tessy Cambridge's husband.

'I should have killed you that day,' he whispered through gritted teeth. 'I should have killed you.'

He whirled, slammed a fist into the wall. Christ, he'd never been one to strike out in rage, let his anger control

169

him, but everything inside him suddenly felt unhinged.

Somewhere in the depths of his mind he heard his brother's voice urging calm, but it had little effect. A monster was loose, and he would get away with it if Jim didn't find him and put a bullet between his eyes.

He drew a deep breath, struggling to get control of his temper.

He went to the desk, leaned heavily against it, both hands gripping the edges, fingers bleaching.

'I'm sorry, Dan. Sorry I got you killed. It should have been me.'

He swallowed at the emotion knotting in his throat. Somehow he had to make Trask answer for his crimes, but at the moment he was fresh out of options. After the gunfight in the saloon last night, one of the saloon gals had told Jim that Trask had come upstairs and thrown her out of the room. And that she'd heard shots not long after. Jim had gone up to discover Jacob Trask dead and with him likely the last chance at a lead to the outlaw.

'You're always a step behind this bastard,' he mumbled, pushing himself away from the desk. 'He's got you by the balls and he knows it. He's calling the shots.'

Which meant Trask could plan and have the element of surprise on his side again. The outlaw might be anywhere and Jim had little chance of tracking him down unless he made a move.

But that move would likely mean the death of another innocent person and the thought of that made his belly cinch, because that person might just be Spring Treller.

'Where are you?' he yelled suddenly, another burst of rage gripping him. 'Where the hell are you?'

★   ★   ★

By the time night fell Jim was no closer to finding a lead to Jeremy Trask. He'd spent most of the afternoon sifting through Mason's folder on the outlaw and telegraphing nearby towns' lawmen to determine whether there had been any sightings of the bandit. He'd even gone back to Lockeville to see if he could pick up any sign pointing in which direction Trask might have ridden upon leaving. He'd come up empty and with each passing hour his frustration chewed another layer off his nerves.

Diners packed the café by the time he met Spring for supper. He sat across from her, picking at his own meal, not much in the mood for eating.

Spring had just finished her supper of beefsteak and fried red potatoes. The young woman had remained quiet throughout the meal, as had he, adrift in his own churning thoughts. He paused long enough to note she was lovely in the evening kerosene light and under other circumstances he might have lost himself in the feelings starting to take hold deep within him.

'You haven't said much,' Spring said after taking a sip of her coffee. Her blue eyes met his and he frowned.

'Been thinking about Trask almost constantly since he lured us to Lock-eville and killed Dan last night. I'm not used to being on the stalking end of a case. I'm usually the one doing the tracking.'

'He's no ordinary man: he's a monster.'

'No argument from me on that, but I got a notion we don't have a lot of time before he kills again.'

Emotion he couldn't read played on Spring's face. 'Maybe we . . . should just let him go.' She said it in a low voice, as if ashamed. 'Maybe there's things more important.'

'How can you say that?' His tone came harsher than he intended and she drew back in her seat. 'This sonofabitch killed your whole town and my brother. He killed a fine marshal last night as surely as if he had been the one who pulled the trigger.'

'I know.' She bowed her head, then looked up. 'Maybe I'm being selfish, but when I look in your eyes I see something, Jim. I see the hurt and the rage you got for him. He's a monster, like I said, but I'm afraid you'll become one too, just to put him down.'

'That won't happen,' he said, and noted there wasn't anywhere near the conviction in his voice he had hoped there would be. He turned his head to gaze out into the darkened street.

A moment later he felt her hand atop his on the table and it sent a shiver through him. He liked the way her hand felt and for that instant it quelled a measure of the rage burning in his soul.

'I lost as much as anyone, Jim,' she said. 'I lost my husband and my dignity in that town. Then I lost something else when Trask's . . . when Trask's *man* forced me . . . ' She paused, drawing a deep breath. 'I wanted to kill Trask and his gang, 'specially the one who raped me, but now . . . '

He looked back to her, saw the sadness in her eyes.

'Now?'

'I never killed anyone before last night and all I keep seein' in my mind is that man lying on the floor in his own blood.'

'You had no choice, Spring. He would have killed us all.'

She nodded. 'I know. In my mind I saw myself shootin' the one who raped me a hundred times, but killin' in your mind isn't the same as when you actually pull the trigger.'

He gave her a grim smile. 'No, it isn't. But sometimes it's necessary if it saves an innocent life or prevents the deaths of many. Any man who could do what Trask did to Baton Ridge, for whatever reasons he might have built up in his mind, needs to be put down like a rabid coyote.'

She frowned. 'I know you're right. I just . . . maybe after all these months I just wanted something for myself that came without worryin' about it bein' taken away from me.'

He searched her eyes, unsure what

she meant. 'Reckon I don't know what — '

'It's OK, Jim.' She forced a weak smile, then stood. 'Can we go now? Please?'

He nodded, tossed a couple greenbacks on the table. As he grabbed his hat from the seat beside his and stood, he discovered himself strangely reluctant to leave, wanting to spend more time with this young woman. At the moment she was the only thing that quieted a small measure of the rage and vengeance inside him.

They walked back to her hotel in silence and he saw her up to her room. She took the key from her skirt pocket and unlocked the door.

'Reckon I got a notion to get a deputy to stand guard over your room at night,' he said. 'With Trask still out there . . . '

She turned back to him, a resigned expression on her face. 'It isn't necessary. Trask comes to take me here he'll likely come the way he did in

Baton Ridge and a deputy won't make a lick of difference. Reckon he'll plan for something more subtle this time.'

He nodded, knowing she was probably right but suddenly stopped thinking about it as she came up on her toes and kissed him.

He reckoned he'd never felt anything so heavenly, nor tasted anything as sweet. Her lips were soft and full as a fresh peach and the kiss lingered after she pulled back and gazed into his eyes.

A fleeting smile touched her lips. 'I reckon maybe it's a contradiction wanting to be with someone after what happened to me in that alley. But there's a difference between giving something freely and having it taken from you. And I got a notion if Trask does come we might die, so I wanted to tell you what I'm feelin' 'fore that happened. Is there a place for me here, if we come through this, Jim? With you?' She kissed him again.

For a suspended moment everything about Trask and his mission vanished from his mind and only the young woman standing before him filled his thoughts and emotions.

He brushed a strand of hair from her face and she smiled and pressed her cheek against his hand.

Then she drew back and opened her door. 'I ain't ready to . . . to be with a man in that way yet, not after what happened. But I will be, someday. I reckon I'm hopin' you'll be willin' to wait.'

She closed the door before he could answer. He was willing to wait, had no choice but to wait, because no matter the rush of feelings he had for that young woman he had to stop Trask first or there would be no future for either of them.

★   ★   ★

Jeremy Trask cursed the frustration crawling through his nerves. He sat at the rickety table in the shack, a half-empty bottle of whiskey before

178

him. He had a powerful notion to drink the rest and escape his frustration, but goddamned Trallie would probably slit his throat if he passed out drunk.

'They should have come back by now,' he said, his voice low, to Trallie, who was sitting on her bedroll, knees drawn to her chest, arms wrapped about her shins. She hadn't moved much other than to eat or go do her duty outside over the past day. He reckoned she was still holdin' a powerful grudge for what he'd done to her. He'd come to think that gal was never going to be cured of her wicked ways. There was sin and then there was sin, the way he saw it. Killing was justifiable, even righteous, but her peculiar tastes . . .

'Two men should have been enough to take down Darrow and that girl, 'specially seein' as how they had surprise on their side.' Her tone became lifeless, as if she didn't give a damn about anything other than whatever thoughts of killing him were running through her mind.

He shook his head. 'Did they? I reckoned that telegram comin' out of nowhere alerted that manhunter to the fact it was a trap, but I figured on Decker and Trompson being good enough to compensate for that. But the fact they ain't back by now means they ain't comin' back.'

'Then we best pull stakes and head for Mex 'fore Darrow finds us.' She said it without conviction and he saw spite in her eyes. It was just her and him now, and she planned to dissolve that partnership the moment she got the chance. But that's why he had planned for that contingency. If he could count on one thing it would be her betrayal. He had just the notion how to use it.

'No, we stay till Darrow's dead.'

'Why? He ain't nothin' to you. You got your pa and that town. Darrow's damn good at his job. He's too big a risk to play with. Decker and Trompson gettin' their asses kilt proves that.'

He grabbed the whiskey bottle,

jammed it to his lips and swallowed a deep gulp, then slammed the bottle on the table.

'I ran from my pa as a kid and even as a young man, I ever tell you that?' He eyed her and the look on her face said she didn't rightly give a damn.

When she didn't say anything he continued, 'I ain't about to run from no bounty hunter. He and that girl you let escape are the only ends I got left to tie. I aim to do it.'

'How?' Something on her face said she knew she wasn't going to like what might be coming.

He almost laughed. 'You're gonna help me, by payin' that gal a visit tomorrow and taking care of her. I reckon a job like that might get your blood simmerin' . . . '

It was the only way she would take an order now, he reckoned, if he dangled some sugar before the horse.

'What you want me to do?' For the first time in days a lilt came to her voice and he knew he had her.

7

With the next morning, Jim Darrow found himself more conflicted about Jeremy Trask and Spring Treller than he expected. The young woman had awakened things in him he'd never thought existed. After Clay's murder he had lived for one thing only: kill Jeremy Trask the day the sonofabitch walked out of prison.

But now? Now, things weren't as black and white as he'd built them up to be. What if he did just try to live his life and let some other lawman chase down Trask? He could wire the county marshal and ask him to send a posse after the outlaw, wash his hands of the responsibility, then simply let justice take its course.

Trask will come after you and Spring and you know it. He won't just let you walk away. You saw the insane driven

182

look in his eyes that day you brought him in. Killing that whole town proved it. He won't leave things unfinished.

That was a sticking point, wasn't it? That and the fact that if he didn't do everything in his power to destroy the monster who'd butchered an entire town he would not be able to live with himself.

Something else figured into the equation or he might have indeed decided to let the law handle it and let justice take its course. What if Trask somehow escaped a hangman's noose again? Spring could link one of his gang to Baton Ridge, and others in Lockeville had witnessed Trask kill. Although some of the evidence was circumstantial, they still had enough to assure the outlaw a necktie party. But after what had happened a year ago in court, could Jim take that chance? Could he risk some fancy lawyer somehow getting Trask a prison sentence instead of a death sentence? Not only would that pose a possible future danger to

Spring, but it would mean Clay might not rest in peace.

Clay wouldn't want you to get yourself killed. He'd want you to take a chance with her, go on with your life and quit this business.

'I can't do that, Clay,' he whispered. 'I can't let him go free and I can't let anything happen to that girl . . . '

Way he saw it, that left him no choice. Too much was at stake and too much anger seethed within him to just stand back and let things ride.

Jim sighed as he walked along the boardwalk towards the café where he and Spring met for breakfast every morning. He would be a few minutes late, but upon leaving his small home at the edge of town he'd first stopped at the church to talk to one of the women about setting Spring up with a room and some sort of job working for the preacher.

He hoped the good news would buffer her reaction to the decision he'd come to.

Nerves fluttered in his belly as he reached the café and entered. He spotted her sitting at a corner table near the back. For the first time since he'd brought her to this town she appeared much more relaxed, the look on her face brighter. It looked natural on her, made her even lovelier.

He doffed his hat, tossed it on the next chair, then sat. A waitress took their order and sauntered away, returning a short time later with a pot of coffee.

'Reckon I thought of a hundred things to say to you after last night,' Spring said, a wisp of a smile on her lips. 'But none of them seemed especially right, because maybe I made a fool of myself being so forward.'

The memory of her kiss brought a surge of warmth to his innards. 'You didn't make a fool of yourself. I thought about it, too. Reckon that's why I came to a few decisions.' He saw her mood change instantly, as if she'd been expecting disappointment.

'I'm used to being let down,' she said, voice low. 'Maybe I assumed something that wasn't there.'

'It isn't like that. It's about Trask, and how we go on from this point.'

She uttered a nervous chuckle. 'Just say it, that's the best way. I can't live with uncertainty anymore.'

He nodded. 'You don't have to. I talked to a lady at the church. There's a room and job waitin' for you when you want it till you get back on your feet. She said they could teach you dress-makin' skills, or some such.'

She took a sip of her coffee, her expression unchanging, her body rigid, as if braced for the worst. The reaction puzzled him. He had expected the news to make her happy. He had damn little experience with women and it occurred to him now he was like to say something totally dumb-assed and not realize it until it was too late.

Her head lifted and a question showed in her eyes. 'I appreciate that, Jim, really I do. But I'm wondering what else you've got on your mind? It sounds like you're settin' me up to survive on my own and that means . . .' She let the words trail off.

'What happened last night . . .' He searched for the words, finding the right ones elusive. 'What happened last night was something I never expected. I never had a place for a woman in my life. I always reckoned what I did for a livin' was too dangerous. I've made plenty of enemies, some I don't even know about, ones lookin' to take down a manhunter just to earn their notches.'

'You sayin' there's no place for me in your life? That your answer?' Her tone hardened, laced with dread, and he knew he was doing a damn poor job of relating his feelings.

'What I'm sayin' is Trask is too dangerous and I won't have you risking your life. I've got enough blood on my conscience with Clay and Dan's.'

'He won't give me a choice, Jim. You know that. He's comin' for me no matter what I do. We killed two of his men.'

'I reckon you're right.'

'And I know I said last night maybe we should just let him go, but I realized you were right. I can't let go what his . . . what happened to me. I can't have a normal life until I know Trask can't hurt either of us or anyone else.'

He nodded, taking a sip of his own coffee, then let out a long sigh. 'I thought about what you said, too. Thought about just letting the law handle him. But you're right, he *will* come after us. And my brother deserves justice.' He paused, glancing out the window, unable to look her in the eye. 'That's why I'm goin' after him and his man alone. I aim to call down the county marshal to protect you while I'm gone, so if I don't come back you'll be safe.'

His gaze went back to her and the anger that flashed across her face told him the news hit just about the way he expected it to.

'You think I just need some Galahad to protect me? After what I've been through I'm as strong as any man, and I can kill again if I have to to protect my own.'

Again he struggled to find the right words, but again they eluded him. He'd always seen women as things a fella put on a pedestal, something to be cherished and protected and maybe as easily broken by the careless words of a mule-headed man such as himself. But they weren't that way and in many ways the woman before him was stronger than he was himself. She'd come through hell and wasn't about to give up, while he'd wallowed in self-pity for the better part of a year since his brother's murder.

'That ain't what I meant. I don't want anything to happen to you.'

'And if you go off and get yourself killed, what then? I lose someone else and just try to go on thinkin' there's a goddamned life for me? Or wait for Trask to come finish the job? Because if he kills you I'll be next on his list and no county marshal will be able to stop him. A whole town couldn't stop him. He's got at least one more with him, maybe others. You don't know what you're walkin' in to any more than you did when Mason got killed. But I know. You're walkin' into death.'

His stubborn streak set in, making him plant his feet. 'I won't risk your life — '

'My life's — our *lives* are already at risk whether I go after him with you or not.'

'My mind's made up, Spring. You're stayin' here under the law's protection.'

'You got no right to decide for me!' Her voice climbed in pitch and volume and the waitress cast them a disapproving glance. He nodded to her that everything was all right, but it wasn't, was it? He was just digging his hole deeper and Spring was getting angrier by the second.

'You asked me the other night if I had a deathwish; I reckon I might ask you the same thing. Dan Mason was an experienced lawman and he still got his ticket punched. What chance do you think you have?'

Her eyes narrowed and her brow furrowed. 'I've got survival on my side. I didn't come through months of hunger and grief and that attack on the town only to lose everything again. What I went through made me stronger. It made me see those folks turning their backs on others not as fortunate as themselves were plain wrong and I don't have to be that way. I won't let Trask kill anyone else.'

He shook his head, his mouth suddenly bone dry. 'I can't risk it.'

Her eyes flamed. 'Like I said, that choice isn't yours.'

'The hell it ain't. You're stayin' here! Ridin' on the trail of a vicious killer is no place for a woman and I won't have you slowin' me down.' He made his words as harsh as he could, only half meaning them but wanting to keep her from getting herself killed more than he wanted to prevent her from growing angrier with him.

Scarlet flooded her cheeks and she bolted to her feet, knocking into the table, upsetting her cup and spilling coffee. 'Maybe you best just say what you really mean, Mr. Darrow. Maybe the trail isn't any place for some dirty little whore who lives on the street and begs men to take care of her. Maybe you reckon I'm just lookin' to be *your* whore, is that it?'

'That ain't what I meant,' he countered, her words stinging, making emotion ball in his throat. Jesus, why was he mussing this all up?

Her glare pierced him. 'Oh, no? Then just what did you mean? Tell me, because I reckon you got some all-fired gentle way of puttin' it to make me think I actually mean somethin' to you.'

'I . . . ' Oh, Christ, he didn't know what to say without making it worse. Heat flooded his face and he stared at her stupidly, searching for something, anything that would convince her to stay behind and ease her mind that she was more to him than just some charity case or wanton woman he was looking to saddle.

She stared at him, pain lancing her eyes, lips quivering. 'I'm falling in love with you, Jim, if that means anything. I'm not a whore and I'm not some timid little woman lookin' to be taken care of. Maybe once I figured myself to be helpless, but now . . . now I know who I am. I got a choice and I choose to go with you after Trask. You won't stop me.' With that, she spun and ran from the café and he sat there like an idiot, watching her go.

* * *

Spring ran all the way back to the hotel, holding back tears. Maybe she had let her guard down too soon with the first person to be kind to her; maybe she had trusted a man she still didn't fully know and risked her heart too much. What did Jim Darrow really think of her? How did he see a woman who was living on the street one day then asking him about the possibility of a future the next?

'You stupid little fool,' she chastized herself, a tear slipping from her eye.

You're just jumping to conclusions, she told herself. He's just trying to protect you.

But what good would it do if he went off and got himself killed? She could survive on her own again, she knew that; now she had options she hadn't in Baton Ridge. But was just surviving enough anymore? Wasn't life more than that? Didn't it come with a chance at some small measure of happiness?

When she reached the hotel, she yanked open the door, then ran up the stairs that flanked the back wall to the upper level. When she reached the top, she paused, hand on the rail. She drew a deep breath, shaking her head, berating herself for overreacting.

She wasn't being fair. He deserved the benefit of the doubt. She was just hypersensitive because of all she'd been through over the past few months. If he saw her as a whore he would never have helped her, spent so much time with her or wanted to keep her out of harm's way so badly. That kiss last night had been real; she'd felt the passion in him.

Things were just spinning through her mind and heart too fast and she had to give herself some time to calm down. Then they could discuss things rationally. He could not go after Trask and that outlaw gal alone and he would just have to accept that. Whether it was with county marshal men or a town posse, she would ride with him.

'You won't stop me from following you,' she said through clenched teeth. 'You won't stop me from savin' you from yourself, no matter what you might think of me.'

She pushed herself from the rail and went down the hall, arms wrapped about herself.

When she reached her door, she stopped and fished the key from her skirt pocket. She noticed her hands trembling as she inserted it into the lock. She swung the door open and stepped inside, her heart pounding in her ears and emotion clogging her throat.

An instant later everything inside her froze. As she swung the door shut she saw a woman, standing with her back pressed to the wall, a gun in her hand. The same woman who had forced herself upon her in the alley the day Trask and his men rode into Baton Ridge.

The woman smiled a rattlesnake smile. 'Miss me, sugar?' she asked.

'You!' Spring yelled. Thoughts clouded by rage, she acted on pure instinct and without regard to her life. She slammed a foot into the outlaw woman's shin and the girl screeched a word Spring had never heard come out of a woman.

The gun wavered and Spring threw herself at the outlaw, grabbing the boyish woman's gun arm and clamping a hand about her wrist.

The outlaw woman was strong, nearly as strong as a man, and it was all Spring could do to hold on to her. She jerked up a knee, powered it into the outlaw woman's thigh. The woman let out a bleat of pain and another curse. Spring wasted no time slamming the outlaw's hand back against the wall. The Smith & Wesson flew from the woman's grip and hit the floor without discharging, spinning halfway across the room.

'What the hell are you doin', you stupid bitch?' the outlaw woman screamed, struggling to force Spring backward.

'You ain't takin' me again,' Spring said, through gritted teeth, every ounce of her rage flowing into her strength. She hoped it would be enough, but she suddenly stumbled as the woman forced her back. She went over backward and down, the outlaw woman landing on top of her.

The outlaw woman laughed, poised atop Spring. 'You want it rough this time, honey? Old Trallie's just right fine with that.'

'Get the hell off me!' Spring tried to buck the woman off but the outlaw was too strong. Trallie forced Spring's arms against the floor, holding her down, then pressed her face close. Spring turned her head to avoid Trallie's searching lips. She felt the other woman's hot breath against her cheek.

'Surprised to see me?' Trallie asked. 'I reckoned Darrow would put you up at the hotel, but the desk man was downright inhospitable when it came to giving out your room number. Dumb sonofabitch got more talkative right before I killed him, though.'

Spring's belly plunged. 'You and Trask . . . you're gonna hang for what you done.'

Trallie uttered a laugh devoid of humor. 'Now you listen to me, you stupid bitch, and listen good. I came here to tell you and your bounty man somethin' that would help — '

Before she got any further, a knock sounded on the door.

*   *   *

Jim paid for the coffee, then headed from the café after sitting there a good five minutes wondering how the hell he had turned something that was supposed to help Spring Treller into horseflop.

He'd never once thought of her as a whore or someone looking just to escape her present situation. Anyone could see in her eyes she was too proud, too strong for that.

'You stupid bastard,' he scolded himself, as he headed down the boardwalk towards the hotel. In his bull-headed desire to protect her he'd only managed to make everything worse. He had only known her a few days but in that short time he reckoned she'd become the most important thing in his life, maybe even more important than killing Jeremy Trask.

He had to go to her, explain things somehow, though Christa'mighty with his skill with words he was likely to do more harm than good. But he couldn't let her go on thinkin' he'd meant something he hadn't. And maybe that would come down to risking her life by letting her track Trask and his man with him, the way it had risked Dan Mason's.

He didn't like the idea but he had a notion she wasn't going to give him a choice or pay any attention to his orders. Maybe he liked that about her too and maybe in the end he could protect her better if she came with him.

He reached the hotel, entered, his belly doing a doe-si-doe as he went to the stairs at the back of lobby. He reckoned going after outlaws in his manhunting days was easier than thinking of a way to apologize to Spring Treller, but he'd best come up with something right fast if he expected to calm her down.

Two minutes later, he reached her

room and lifted his hand to knock. His hand stopped mid-air as a sound came from within. The sound had come from something heavy hitting the floor and every nerve in his body tightened. His hand, in motion again, swept to the Peacemaker at his side and pulled it from its holster. With his left hand he knocked on the door.

'Spring?' he said. 'It's Jim. Open the door!'

A yell came in answer.

★ ★ ★

With the sound of the knock Trallie's head swept around and her face tightened into a mask of anger. 'Goddammit, your fella's got piss-poor timin'!' she said in a hiss, as Jim's voice followed a second behind the knock.

Trallie scrambled off Spring and leaped for the gun on the floor a few feet away.

The outlaw grabbed the Smith & Wesson and swung it towards the door.

Spring's heart jumped and she knew she'd never reach the woman before she pulled the trigger.

'Jim, get away from the door!' Spring shouted, terror in her voice.

Trallie uttered a laugh and pulled the trigger three times.

★　★　★

With Spring's warning shout Jim Darrow reacted instinctively. He leaped to his left just as three bullets punched through the door and buried themselves in the opposite wall.

'Christ!' he whispered, knowing either Trask or the outlaw's man had somehow discovered where Spring was staying and likely been lying in wait when she got back from the café.

Footsteps came from within, the sound of someone running across the room, followed by the grating squeak of window rising.

Jim whirled, snapped out a leg and slammed a boot against the door. The door bounded inward with a splintering of wood about the latch. He glimpsed a figure climbing through the window across the room.

Spring was on the floor, on her hands and knees, but appeared OK.

Jim fired twice at the vanishing figure, taking splinters out of the window frame but missing the retreating outlaw.

He ran into the room, paused to help Spring to her feet, then went to the window. An outside stairway ran from the window to the street. The outlaw, who had already reached the bottom, bolted along the side of the building towards a horse tethered a block down.

Jim swung a foot through the window and dropped down on to the stairway landing. Gun held close to his cheek, eyes roving to make sure Trask wasn't hidden somewhere below to back up his man, he bounded down the stairs.

Spring came through the window after him; he heard her clomping down the steps behind him, not entirely happy she was exposing herself to possible danger.

The outlaw reached his horse and jumped into the saddle as quick as any rodeo rider Jim had ever seen. He put on speed, bolting out into the street, heart pounding in his throat. Desperate to stop the outlaw, he leveled his Peacemaker; if that fella got away any lead to Trask went with him.

With no time to aim, he fired, praying he got lucky. Two bullets missed but the third kicked the outlaw sideways out of the saddle.

The shot hit the outlaw's shoulder; it shouldn't have been enough to kill him, but the rider got an ankle caught in the stirrup going down and his body twisted under the horse. The animal's hoofs pounded into his chest, likely shattering ribs and innards alike. His foot pulled free of the stirrup and the mount kept running.

The outlaw lay on his face, unmoving, afterward.

Folks, shock on their faces, stopped

along the boardwalks and peered at the body. Jim slipped his Peacemaker into his holster. Even from where he stood he could tell the outlaw no longer posed a threat.

'This man tried to kill this woman,' he said to folks casting him horrified looks. They nodded, anxiety easing from their features. Most in Orchard Pass knew him by sight and realized without a marshal at the moment he was the next best thing. By the time Jim reached the body, a few others had gathered around it. He knelt as Spring came up behind him.

Blood had pooled beneath the outlaw, flowing both from the shoulder wound and from beneath the shirt where the hoofs had done their work, and was soaking into the dirt. Jim flipped the body over and felt for a pulse, but even before glancing at the crushed-in chest, he knew this fellow would never lead them to Trask now.

He let go of the wrist, looked back to

Spring and shook his head. She knelt beside him.

'That's the one who raped me . . . ' A strange hitch hung in her voice and she appeared almost afraid to tell him. His gaze narrowed as he looked back to the body. Somehow the outlaw had retained his hat and it was jammed half over his face. Jim pulled it away from the outlaw's dead features, his brow cinching.

'That's — '

'A woman.' Spring said. 'I was afraid to tell you.'

'Jesus . . . ' whispered Jim.

'She held a gun to me, made me . . . ' Her voice wavered. He stood, helped her up, then took her into his arms.

'It's all right, Spring, she's dead. She won't be hurtin' you ever again.'

'It isn't all right.' Her tone hardened. 'But I reckon she got what she deserved.'

He sighed. 'Trask must have sent her to kill you.'

Spring pulled back, shook her head.

'I don't think he did. She said something about coming to help us while she was attacking me. She didn't have to say that.'

He nodded and knelt again, studying the body, a dark feeling swelling inside him. Death was never pretty and no matter how many times he saw it he reckoned he'd never get used to it, even if it were deserved.

'Reckon she won't be telling us nothin' now . . . ' He stopped, words trailing off, brow knitting.

'What is it?' Spring asked.

He peered at the dead woman's feet. 'That silvery substance on her boot . . . ' He didn't touch it. He recognized what it was from when he and Clay had done some tracking work for a silver mine company robbed by one of its own men.

'What is it?'

'Think it's mercury.'

'How does that have anything to do with Trask?'

'They use mercury to separate silver

from ore. Melts it. It's right poison, I hear.'

Understanding drifted across Spring's face. 'There's an abandoned silver mine about a twenty minute ride from Baton Ridge.'

Jim stood. 'Maybe it's a long shot, but way I see it we got no other leads.'

8

Jeremy Trask poised in the shack doorway, gazing out at the late afternoon sunlight-splashed brush and scrabbly ground surrounding the mining camp. As he had expected, Trallie had not returned. Her deceit was as predictable as her abhorrent tastes.

Maybe Trallie was dead; maybe she would come with Darrow to help him finish the job. Whatever the case, he reckoned by now she had told the manhunter just where to find his quarry and that was a contingency for which he had planned.

Darrow and the woman Trallie had let escape were the last pieces of unfinished business that needed to be dealt with before he headed to Old Mex. Oh, the gal technically didn't matter so much anymore, because by now Darrow surely would have informed the county marshal Trask was responsible for the slaughter in Baton Ridge, as well as the murder of two lawmen, an outlaw and Jacob Trask in Lockeville. There were witnesses, enough to get his neck stretched this time; no fancy frock-coated lawyer would be able to keep him out of a noose. But he reckoned if any principles remained in him whatsoever it was that he saw a job to completion once he started it, and that girl would die just because he wanted it that way. Some might have called it an obsession; others might have just said it was the rattlesnake in him.

He called it satisfaction.

He drew a deep breath, folded his arms across his chest, then wandered out on to the rotting porch. His gaze surveyed each patch of brush and bare ground that led into a forest of fir and cottonwood and pine. A trail to the left snaked in the direction of Baton Ridge. He recollected hearing about this mining camp as a kid, how the mine had gone bust when the silver market bottomed, how so many folks from surrounding towns had been left destitute and starving. He remembered laughing about it, reveling in the fact others were suffering as much as he.

The weak perished. That's the way it was in this god-forsaken world. A man survived only on the blood of others. Perhaps fancy men, bankers, lawyers and silver magnates, did it more subtlety with the way they played with lives, caused families to suffer and men to die for personal gain, but they were little different than he. To them, and to him, the lives of others ceased to matter. Long ago, before his father had beaten the last of his humanity out of him, he had worried that everything had gone so dead inside. Now he no longer worried; he embraced it. Killing made him feel strong, powerful, in control, the way he had never been allowed to feel under his pa's rule. And the more he killed the stronger he felt.

That feeling was an addiction, and like any other — whiskey, whores, gambling — it wore off fast and with it came a terrible compulsion that threatened to make him look inside his soul, see the emptiness there. He reckoned it was a damn good thing the West was full of victims, because little stood between that revelation and a bullet to the brain.

He sighed, the moment of reflection passing as the thought of the manhunter occupied his mind again. He reckoned he didn't have a lot of time. Darrow was likely already on his way, perhaps even with the girl.

Darrow wanted revenge this time. That manhunter wasn't going to leave it up to the courts. He knew damn well who was responsible for his brother's death, no matter what the lawyer had claimed and the judge had accepted.

He also had seen the slaughter in Baton Ridge and knew Trask was too dangerous to leave alive.

Would Darrow bring the law with him? Trask doubted it, not if the manhunter intended to kill him the way he suspected. But it would pay to have extra dynamite planted just in case.

Trask uttered a vacant laugh and stepped down to the ground. He went to where heavy brush had overgrown the mouth of the old mine and swept it aside with a whisk of his arm.

As he stepped through the opening, damp coolness that felt like the embrace of death splashed his face. A grim smile pulled at his lips. Death, indeed.

He pulled a lucifer from his pocket and snapped it against his belt buckle. The match flared, throwing sulfur light over the shaft interior. His gaze focused on a crate to his left, one labeled DYNAMITE. Old stuff, likely touchy as hell, if it were sweating nitro. He would have to be careful while arranging his little surprise or the stuff might save Darrow the trouble of killing him.

* * *

Jim guided the horses out of the livery stable after saddling them, a bay and a roan. He stopped just beyond the double doors, noticing Spring standing on the boardwalk across the street, peering at him. He hadn't said much to her since killing the outlaw who'd raped her, and frankly he was at a loss for words. Anything he might have said seemed woefully inadequate, and right now he needed to focus on the man he now suspected was holed up in a mine outside of Baton Ridge.

He waved her over and she came slowly, as if unsure of herself now, unsure how he'd react, whether he'd try to stop her from riding with him.

'I saddled both horses for a reason,' he said as she reached him. 'I reckon I got no right to tell you what to do. You want to go with me, there's a horse and a rifle for you.'

She nodded, a thin smile flickering on her lips. 'I want to go.'

She bowed her head, as if ashamed to look at him.

He sighed, hoping for once he'd say the right thing. 'Who did it to you don't matter, Spring. It was wrong and you got nothing to be ashamed of. She won't be doin' it to anyone else.'

Spring nodded, not looking up, then climbed into the saddle.

Jim stepped up on to his own mount and reined around. He gigged the horse into a fast gait, Spring following suit. The ride was a good two and a half hours and he aimed to cut a measure off that.

They rode in silence, the miles falling way and with each that passed his belly tightened. A little over a year ago Jeremy Trask had murdered Clay and at last the day of reckoning had come. This time one of them would die. He prayed the woman at his side would live to get the chance at life she so richly deserved. She'd been through hell and though bringing her along went against his better judgement he was forced to admire her courage more than he already did.

Two hours on, he slowed his mount to a brisk walk and angled right of

Baton Ridge — he had no desire to ride through the town and force her to relive any of the memories that came with it.

He glanced at her, a certain heaviness of fate weighing on his soul, knowing the next half-hour would determine whether his life began or ended. If it ended, he decided he wasn't going to his grave leaving things unsaid.

'I didn't mean what you thought I meant earlier.'

She peered at him, her features pinched, her eyes hard but worried. 'I know you didn't. I reckon I've just had so much go bad I was lookin' to run from something good before it had a chance to disappoint me.'

He frowned. 'Trask might kill us both. He's smart enough to know that when his girl doesn't come back something went wrong and she might have left a trail back to him.'

She nodded. 'I know that too, but he won't give up till he kills us. At least this way we go in with our eyes open.'

'Reckon it's better than bein' taken

unprepared.' He went silent, one hand going to the Peacemaker at his hip, the desire to kill a man never as powerful as it was at that moment.

'I'm fallin' in love with you, Jim,' Spring said. 'I know I said it already at the café, but I wanted to say it again in case we — '

He peered at her, a thin smile on his lips, and nodded. 'We're comin' out of this, Spring. Just keep that in your mind.'

A grim expression told him she heard the doubt in his voice.

'Trask might be expectin' us,' she said.

'Wouldn't wager against it.'

'He might have other men.'

'He might.' As they neared the mining area he suddenly regretted giving her the choice to come along. But persuading her to go back was out of the question and he knew it.

You don't need vengeance, Brother, he heard Clay say in his mind. *Justice will do.*

'I'm sorry, Clay,' he whispered. 'Justice ain't enough.'

Spring looked at him, concern on her face. 'You all right?'

He nodded. 'Reckon. Just thinkin' about something my brother would have told me about needin' justice instead of revenge. Think he would have been wrong.'

'I reckoned that with the gal who raped me, Jim. Even with her dead now I don't feel any different. Time's the only thing that takes care of that, not killin'.'

He gave her a grim smile, then centered his gaze ahead. 'Reckon I'm fallin' in love with you too . . . ' he whispered.

Another mile on the woods thickened and the trail thinned. The terrain became hilly, peppered with boulders and deadfalls.

'Mine's not far ahead,' Spring ducked her chin forward.

He nodded and slowed his horse. 'We best take it on foot the rest of the way.

He won't hear us comin' that way.'

'What if he has guards posted?' she asked, slowing her own horse and jumping off.

'We'll keep our eyes open. I got a notion he sure as hell has something planned.'

They tethered their mounts to a branch and Spring slipped the Winchester out of its saddle-boot, gripping it in bleached fingers.

He drew his own gun and started forward, angling to the side of the trail. Eyes roving, senses alert, he spotted the abandoned shack about a hundred feet ahead, as the trail widened slightly. He noted where branches and brush had been hacked away, confirming the place was recently occupied. He spotted a horse to the right, Trask's stolen mount, if he figured right.

'He's here,' Jim whispered and Spring nodded.

'Don't see any guards.'

Jim shook his head. 'You wouldn't if they're good. That's why I want you to stay behind and cover my back while I go on ahead.'

'I don't — ' She started to protest, but he gave her a sharp look.

'Trask has something in store and there's no telling what. No sense in him trapping both of us with it and if there are any guards I need you in a position to stop them from back-shootin' me.'

She studied his face, as if trying to determine whether the deathwish she had accused him of having was real, then nodded and lifted the Winchester. She angled behind a tree as Jim started forward in a crouch, his Peacemaker held at his cheek in readiness.

Eyes roving, he spotted nothing to indicate a presence at the shack or guards lurking in the surrounding woods. Everything seemed deathly quiet, even the forest animals silent. He noted the clump of brush covering the old mining shaft, wondered if Trask might be waiting inside, a rifle trained on the trail. He caught no glint of sunlight on steel, no hint of movement, but after what had happened in Lockeville, he kept his guard up anyway. Trask was too clever to misread again.

He spotted no other horses, strengthening his conjecture Trask was now alone.

He crept closer to the shack, eyes in a squint as he tried to spot some sign of the outlaw.

'That's far enough, manhunter,' a voice came and ice trickled down his spine. He recognized that voice from the trial a year ago; it was burned into his mind, and with it came a wave of hatred.

'Trask!' Jim yelled. 'I've come to take you in.'

A laugh answered his statement. 'The hell you have, Darrow. You've come to kill me for putting that no-good brother of yours out of my misery.'

The words sent fury surging through his veins and he nearly made the damn fool mistake of rushing the cabin. Only the fact he wasn't entirely certain where the voice was coming from held him back and likely saved him from getting his hide filled with lead.

Forcing himself to keep his composure, his gaze went back to the busted windows. There, in the second one — a rifle barrel rested on the sill.

'Toss your gun backward, Darrow, then stand right still.'

He calculated his odds of leaping sideways and avoiding getting drilled by lead while getting off his own shot. His thoughts must have bled on to his face.

''Fore you consider shootin' your way out of this, Mr Darrow, kindly look to your right and left, in the clumps of brush you're standin' between.'

Jim's gaze automatically cut in both directions. 'Christ,' he mumbled. It dawned on him then the outlaw's rifle wasn't aimed at him but at one of the bundles of dynamite. Sweat beaded on the sticks; the slightest jar would set them off. Even if he tried to dive sideways and trigger a shot, Trask's bullet would find a bundle and blow him straight to his Maker.

''Course, you don't know which bundle I'm aimin' at, Darrow, so you got a fifty-fifty chance of jumpin' the right way, 'less I can adjust my aim fast enough. You want to take that wager?'

Jim's breath caught in his lungs. His gaze went straight ahead, wondering if a leap backward or forward might take him out of harm's way. He doubted it.

As if in answer to his thought, Trask's voice came again. 'You're thinking of jumping forward or backward, there's more bundles, all of them concealed where you won't spot them before I can pull the trigger. Reckon here's where I should tell you I'm a dead shot.'

He was caught. Again. Like in Lockeville, only the odds were worse this time. A low curse came from his lips and he saw any chance of punishing the outlaw for his brother's death dissolving. Worse than that, Spring would have no chance against Trask once the outlaw killed him.

'What do you want, Trask? I reckon

223

you've got no intention of letting me walk out of here alive.'

'I want you to toss your gun back, Mr. Darrow. An' be gentle about it. We don't want any accidental bangs, now, do we?'

He saw damn little choice. Every trail led to death. He lowered his gun, then tossed it straight backward. It landed a few feet away in the sand.

The shack door opened a second later and Jeremy Trask stood in the entryway, a demon in a duster holding a Winchester. As Trask stepped across the porch, his duster swung back to reveal a Smith & Wesson at his hip.

'Figured you wouldn't give up the hunt, Darrow,' Trask said, stepping down to the ground.

'You figured right.' His palms began to sweat and beads of perspiration sprang out on his forehead.

Trask smiled. 'You come alone?'

Jim had to make his lie sound convincing. 'I hadn't, some lawman would have picked you off the moment you stepped out that door.'

The statement made Trask pause and Jim could tell the outlaw knew he had made a potential mistake. Had a lawman been hiding in wait, the outlaw would have died right then and there and he knew it.

'What about the girl? Where is she?'

'Leave her out of this.'

Trask shook his head, stepping closer to Jim. 'Can't do that. See, I'm just one mean sonofabitch and I got this thing about leavin' loose ends. She's a loose end.'

Trask suddenly reversed the rifle in his hands and swung it upward in a short arc. The butt slammed into Jim's chin. Pain cracked through his jaw and his senses wavered.

The outlaw stepped backward as Jim fell forward and landed on the ground on his hands and knees. Blood streamed from his mouth, dripping into the sand.

'What'd you figure on doin' once you got here, manhunter?' Trask asked, voice taunting. 'Killin' me by your lonesome? You think I knew Trallie wouldn't lead you back to me?'

Jim looked up at him, came up on to his knees. 'Your gal's dead, Trask.'

The outlaw uttered a low laugh. 'Makes no nevermind. Fact, saves me the trouble of killin' her myself.'

A skritching sound came and Trask's gaze lifted. Jim glanced sideways to see Spring standing a dozen feet diagonally in back of him, her Winchester aimed at Trask's chest.

'S'pose you just drop your rifle slowlike,' she said, determination and anger on her face.

Trask gazed at Jim, annoyance in his dull eyes. 'Never figured you as one to risk an innocent gal's life, Darrow.'

'Reckon that's your second mistake.'

Trask laughed, the expression more mocking this time. 'Don't matter. It's the third that gets ya killed.'

'Won't take a third if you don't do what I tell you,' Spring said, jamming the Winchester butt into her shoulder and levering a shell into the chamber.

Trask's gaze returned to Jim, and his rifle aim shifted a couple of inches. 'You won't shoot me, missy.'

Spring's eyes narrowed. 'The hell I won't! You can't get that rifle up in time to fire at me and my finger's already on the trigger. I don't rightly relish the thought of killin' a man again but the next bullet out of this rifle has your name on it.'

'Does it? Take a good look at where my rifle's aimed. I reckon my next bullet's got that bundle of dynamite's name on it. You could shoot me, but I'd still pull the trigger and your fella would die with me.'

Spring's hands began to shake and Jim knew she would never risk his life, even if he told her to just kill Trask and save the lives he might potentially kill. The rifle lowered.

'Toss it in the bushes,' Trask ordered.

Spring complied, her face going pale, defeat in her eyes. She knew it meant death for them both.

Trask gave Jim a cocky sneer.

'Reckon I ain't the trusting sort after all, eh, Darrow?'

The outlaw lifted his rifle and aimed at Spring.

'No!' Jim shouted, panic seizing him. He jumped to his feet, his only thought to save Spring's life, even if it meant throwing both himself and the outlaw on to the dynamite.

Trask jerked the rifle back, trying to brain Jim as he hurled himself against the outlaw. Legs still shaky, the move was awkward and got him a glancing rifle blow to the temple that made the world about him spin. Reacting on instinct, he grappled with the outlaw, throwing punches and kicking at Trask's shins. The move jammed Trask, prevented him from getting his rifle aimed or launching another blow that would have ended the fight.

Jim's vision cleared. He wasted no time arcing a left hook to the outlaw's jaw. Trask staggered, dropped the rifle. Giving the outlaw no time to recover, Jim came at him again, swinging more from rage than skill.

Trask's face washed with a sudden look of terror, and he threw his hands up before his face.

'No, Pa, don't hit me anymore . . . please,' the outlaw mumbled, his eyes suddenly distant, as if he were recollecting something from his past.

Jim charged him, swung an uppercut that took the outlaw flush under the chin and clacked his teeth together with the sound of a gunshot.

Trask's eyes washed blank, then he dropped to his knees.

'I won't do it again, I swear I won't, I swear — ' the outlaw muttered, blood drooling from his mouth, his body shaking.

'What the hell?' Jim said, brow cinching. It was some kind of trick, to get him to let his guard down. It had to be.

Jim bent, grabbed the Smith & Wesson from the outlaw's holster and flung it. It landed in the brush ten feet away.

'I ain't fallin' for it, Trask,' he said, then snapped a boot heel into Trask's face. The outlaw went over backward, lay groaning in the dirt.

Using the back of his hand, Jim swiped blood from his mouth. Fury sent a burst of scarlet into his cheeks. That sonofabitch was going to pay for what he had done to Clay, and to Baton Ridge.

'Get up, you sonofabitch!' Jim yelled. 'Get up and let me avenge my brother.'

Trask's gaze roved aimlessly and unintelligible sounds came from his bloody lips. He drew his knees up to his chest, shuddering.

'Please, Pa, have mercy,' Trask mumbled. 'Please . . . '

Jim watched him, heart pounding, every fiber of his body wanting to pound the bastard to death. But, Christ, maybe Trask wasn't faking, Jim thought. The outlaw seemed somewhere else, some *time* else.

The sonofabitch had lost his mind.

This wasn't the way Jim wanted it to

end. This held no satisfaction, no sense of finality. That man cowering on the ground deserved to die for what he had done.

'No, you ain't gettin' off that easy,' Jim said through clenched teeth. He turned and, avoiding the dynamite, went to his Peacemaker. After picking it up, he turned back to Trask, lifted the gun, bringing it to aim on the outlaw.

'Jim, no,' Spring said, coming up to him and touching his arm. 'He's done. We'll take him back to Orchard Pass and hand him over to the county marshal. Killin' him in cold blood won't bring your brother back.'

'He's lost in his mind, Spring. Courts will put him away in some institution and in a few years . . . '

She shook her head. 'No, not this time. They'll hang him for what he did in Baton Ridge and Lockeville. Others saw him this time.'

Jim's hand shook as he held the gun on the outlaw curled into a mewling ball. He wanted to pull the trigger, wanted to desperately, but where would his humanity be if he killed a defenseless man? Would it bring Clay back? It would have been different if the outlaw had made it self-defense, but like this, like some frightened child . . .

Jim lowered his gun, slid it into its hostler. 'Go back to my horse and fetch the rope. We'll tie him to his horse and bring him back to Orchard Pass.'

Spring nodded, studying his face to make certain he wasn't just sending her away just to have the chance to finish the outlaw. She left him, ran back down the trail.

Jim, keeping his eye on the outlaw, went to the horse tethered to the left and untied it. He handed the reins to Spring after she returned with the rope. He started towards Trask, aiming to tie his hands, then throw him across his horse's saddle.

Trask suddenly unwound from his fetal position, rage and insanity on his face. 'No! You won't hang me!' he screamed. 'Never! You hear me?'

Trask made a dive for the rifle lying a few feet away.

It was his third mistake. Whatever went on in the outlaw's unhinged mind, it clouded his judgement, made him forget about the dynamite he had planted.

Jim saw it in the blink of an eye and reacted nearly as fast. He dove against Spring, hurling her sideways.

As Trask's boot slammed into a bundle of dynamite, the ground erupted in a great upheaval of dust and gravel and blood and ear-shattering noise. Dirt and pieces of the outlaw rained down.

It took Jim and Spring a moment to reach their feet and get their hearing back.

Spring's face had washed three shades paler and her hands went to her cheeks. 'That was — '

'Satisfying?' Jim said before he could stop himself, but even he couldn't shake the nausea spinning in his belly and the sickened feeling in his soul.

'Horrible,' she completed, turning to

him, then sobbing into his chest.

Jim doubted there were enough pieces of Jeremy Trask left for burial.

After long moments, he and Spring went back to their horses in silence. Clay could rest in peace now, he reckoned, and the man he had always figured himself to be was intact, if more because of the young woman at his side than his own sense of restraint. He might have shot Trask in cold blood if she hadn't been there. He might not have. He would never know. But he did know he could go on living now, with Spring, and without the terrible haunting grief he'd lived with for the last year.

THE END

Other titles in the
Linford Western Library:

LAWMEN

Jack Giles

Tom Ford, the sheriff of Stanton, was gunned down while trying to keep the peace between the hands of rival ranches. News of Tom Ford's death reaches his son, Chris, and Marshal Sam Ward while they are hunting down a killer. Chris returns home to face his past and to find his father's killer and for this he must take up his father's badge — only to discover that not everything is as it seems . . .

BLOOD CREEK

Lance Howard

Fifteen years earlier five unruly sons had committed a heinous crime against a young Ute woman, and walked away unpunished. But now a ruthless killer is stalking those boys. Bent on revenge he's murdering their wives and, piece by piece, destroying their lives. After manhunter Calin Travers is attacked, then lured to Sundown, Colorado, he discovers himself face to face with guilt from the past and a vengeful killer who has marked him for death.

KID DYNAMITE

Michael D. George

Government agent Scott Taylor arrives in Adobe Wells to tackle the corruption which is rife. But Cody Carter has other plans. He's ruled Franklin County for years with an army of outlaws and Cheyenne warriors to do his killing for him. Forewarned of Taylor's mission, Carter sends out his top gunman to stop the agent. Scott doesn't know that Kid Dynamite is waiting to kill him in his own evil way and looks as if he is doomed.

BLOOD ON THE SKY

Elliot Long

Will Hopkirk is settled for good with Diaglito's White Mountain Apaches and his beautiful Apache wife Sonseray. But then Diaglito is devastated when Tobias Hatch kills his young son, Choate. And white man's justice outrages Diaglito when it finds Hatch not guilty. The war chief vows that white man's blood must spill to satisfy the wrong done to him and his people. Now Hopkirk must choose where his loyalties lie, as the frontier erupts into a rage of violence.

SHOWDOWN AT DANE'S BEND

Jack Holt

Sam Limbo, innocent but jailed for murder, is forced to remain in Dane's Bend, a powder-keg town. The townsfolk are awaiting the arrival of the notorious Donovan brothers, intent on avenging the killing of the youngest Donovan. The brothers have a big interest in the bank which, with a secret stash, has taken on hired private security. Limbo breaks out of jail, but returns, lured by the marshal's daughter. And it's Limbo who saves the town that wanted to hang him.